I was never COOL

I was never COOL

~

Joseph Musso Jr.

Goldfish Press

Published by
Goldfish Press, Seattle
202 6th Ave. South, Suite 1105
Seattle, WA 98104-2303

Book design by Karen Johnson, Level 29 Design

Manufactured in the United States of America

ISBN 0971160155
Library of Congress Catalog Card Number 2006930523

this book is for my father

I would like to thank Koon Woon,
my editor and my friend.

Stories from this collection have
appeared in the following publications:

"Roommate" in *Chrysanthemum*
"House For Sale" in *Sleepingfish*
"Initiation of the Fat Kid" in *ken*again*
"Trumpet" in *Hobart*

Contents

~

'My mother said it was a shame,
and used the word unique...'

Initiation of
the fat kid

I was never popular in school – even the teachers had it in for me. I remember one day in the third grade, during gym, the class was in the playground. I was on the swings, dormant, and asked the teacher to push me. "No," she said.

She went on to explain that she might hurt herself because I was too heavy, which meant fat. So I "pushed" myself, by swinging my legs until I had worked up enough speed. Later, I saw her pushing the skinny kids.

Ever since, I have disliked teachers.

Call it an initiation.

*

Later that year, I was invited to a birthday party. In the boy's room, at the sinks, he smugly came up to me and said it was a mistake. There were three Joe's in my class. He was one of them and I was one of them. He said, "It wasn't supposed to be you."

When I got home, I told my mother about it.

That night I heard her on the phone, and later of course I didn't go to the party.

*

After school one day, I fell off the monkey bars and tore the skin from under my chin. There was about a four-inch by four-inch wound. I cried, and they called my mother.

I wore a bandage for a while, and was famous in class. At first, when kids would ask, I told them I was in a fight with three fifth graders. I told them I saved a baby bird from a cut-throat mob of tabby cats. I told them I jumped off the roof of my house like Tarzan.

I told them, I told them, I told them.

I was a star.

The cute girl in class came up. She rubbed my arm, and wanted to sit next to me. She smiled.

Then, another kid ruined it for me. "He fell off the monkey bars," he told everybody.

*

I was walking home from school one day. A girl in the eighth grade began teasing me. She used my last name as if I were a bug. I threw a stone.

At home, crying, I threw myself on the bed. My mother saw, and asked me what happened. When I told her, she read to me from the bible.

Somehow, I felt better.

*

Years later, when I was in my twenties and in my prime, I saw that same girl in a luncheonette. She was waiting tables. It had been a long time, and at first she didn't recognize me. When she came up to my table with a menu, my penis was hard.

I asked her, "Do you remember me?"

She squinted, and finally said, "You're the boy I used to tease."

I was curious about her, and mentioned the motel around the corner. She said, "I'm not desperate, you know."

We didn't go to the motel, but I left a big tip. Somehow, it felt like I had just paid for sex. She watched me leave, and scraped the money off the table. I wondered how many kids she had, and how old they were.

And if she teased them until they ran home crying.

*

I saw that teacher again too, the one who wouldn't push me in the swing. Life sometimes has a way of completing the picture. The rocks in your life, the ones you stumbled over, often end up in front of you again.

You can either stumble again, or step over.

It was at a wedding for a friend I hadn't seen in years. When I received the invitation, I asked my girlfriend at the time if she wanted to go. I told her, "There's an open bar."

The teacher was older, and had gained weight. She seemed so young back then, just a child herself. My girlfriend got drunk and went over to her table. Slurring her words, she told Teacher, "You should see him in bed!"

I loved it.

⋆

Later, when it was time to toss the bouquet, my girlfriend embarrassed herself. In front of everyone, I picked her up off the floor. A dog had gotten into the hall, an Irish Setter. I held out a hand.

My girlfriend came to.

One of them nipped my finger.

⋆

Roommate

 My first roommate would walk around in his underwear, and burst through my bedroom door when I was trying to sleep.

I was twenty years old.

Once, I came home and found him reading my private notebooks. He was squatted in the middle of the floor, reading intently. Caught off guard, he said, "Wait! I'll make you a drink."

The drink was strong, and the day had been tough. I relaxed.

Later, when I pressed him, he said, "I was looking for you."

*

He had a girlfriend who was much younger. She was a junior in high school. He would be on the phone with her every night for hours. Then I found out it was her father on the other end.

*

At Halloween, he was working at a fast-food place. All employees were required to dress up for work. My roommate went as a woman, but not just any woman. The wig was chosen to blend with his skin tone. The glue-on fingernails were long and painted a fiery red.

Matching lipstick, panty hose, expensive high heels, and a form-fitting dress completed the ensemble. He shaved his legs and wore perfume.

He wore the "costume" for several days after Halloween, and then I found out he never worked at a fast-food place.

*

One day, when I got home from work, I found the front door difficult to open. Finally, I pushed it open and was inside. There were several towels jammed against the bottom. The windows too were shut and jammed with towels.

Walking around the apartment, I noticed small pieces of paper placed on all his possessions. I walked up to one and snatched it. It read, "To my brother Charles. Please don't think this is your fault. You taught me this game, and I always loved it."

The note had been taped to a chess set.

His brother Charles liked boys too, and suddenly I wondered which "game" he meant.

Other bits of paper were taped. The birds, still in their birdcage, were left to a niece and nephew. His box of letters from when he was in the Air Force was left to his mother. His Grateful Dead albums he left to his best friend from high school.

As for me, I was left the rent.

I walked around this museum some more. It was hot in the apartment, stifling. I found him in the kitchen, sitting on the floor, drenched in sweat. His head was in his hands.

The oven door was open.

When he looked up, I could see he had been crying. He said, "Don't light a cigaret. This place will go up like the Fourth of July."

*

After trying several hours to talk him out of it, I gave up. I went to a bar where a band I liked was playing. I saw his friend there, the one from high school, the one with the new albums he didn't know about yet. He was wearing a funny hat and smoking a cigaret.

He looked "cool" tapping out the ashes. He bobbed his head to the music.

"Where's Donnie?" he asked.

"In transit," I said.

*

Later in the week, I was sitting with a drink and reading a book. The window was open. I saw my roommate walking up the street. He was soaking wet.

When he was inside, I asked.

Solemnly, he said, "I took a bunch of pills and started swimming out in the ocean. I thought it would be a peaceful way to go."

"What happened?"

"Some kids saved me. They punched me in the stomach until I threw up the pills."

I went back to my book, muttering over the pages, "Fucking kids."

*

In those days, I drank in bars. I stayed out all night. I was too young for consequence.

One groggy morning, I staggered out from my bedroom. When I looked out the window, down in the street, there were three men stealing his car.

I watched with great fascination. The men worked quickly, professionally. There was a precision I admired, a Zen approach to teamwork which made me warm and dizzy.

Finally, an hour or so later, my roommate emerged from his own deep sleep. I said, "Don't look out the window."

When it comes to cars, another word for "stolen" is "repossessed".

*

In January, two of his friends from the Air Force, a married couple, stayed at our apartment. There were telephone calls from strange men. I would answer but have nothing to say. Once, the voice on the other end was a woman's. She asked, "Can you at least tell me if they're alive?"

I said, "They keep eating my food."

We would all watch movies together, and the female would tell the endings because she had seen the movies before. My roommate had a crush on one of them. Days later, all dressed up, they went to Virginia where he testified on their behalf.

I was left in the dark, which I preferred.

When they returned, there was champagne. A glass was put in my hand, and the bubbles tickled my nose. She kissed me on the cheek, and the two boys disappeared. On the couch, she said she liked the way my pants fit. I touched her tongue with my tongue. We smoked weed.

At one point she said, "I have never been afraid of my body. It's the only thing in the world I can trust."

I said, "Look at the music I listen to. Look at the books. I'm not just some fucking guy. I got shit going on."

In the morning all three of them were gone. The phone rang. It was the United States Government. The voice was stern, no-nonsense. It said, "Where are they?"

AWOL is no pretty picture.

I told the voice, just as sternly, "I am naked!"

When the lease was up, we went our separate ways. He still owes me almost three thousand dollars, plus the microwave and the kitchen knives. I haven't seen him since.

Brightly, the words *a bargain* come to mind.

*

Battlefields

My sister once tried to drown me in the pool. She held my head under water until the bubbles stopped zipping to the surface. After that, I refused to bathe. My head was then shoved under the sink and soap was applied. This procedure was repeated with my feet, under my arms, between my legs.

I kicked and screamed.

I never told anyone at school, but the teacher sniffled one day and asked, "Does your mother wash your clothes?"

*

Two neighbor kids and I were playing army. I had a loose tooth. The oldest said, "Stand there and don't move." I did what he said.

He made a fist.

The next thing I knew I was on the ground and my tooth was missing.

They were brothers, and they told me not to tell my mother. So, I didn't. That night I put the tooth under my pillow. Since I didn't tell my mother about it, there was no money in the morning. That's how I learned the truth about the Tooth Fairy.

Another time the youngest of the brothers threw a baseball as hard as he could, right at my head. I ducked in time and the ball put a dent in my father's car instead.

*

I liked to play army as a kid. The outcome was rigged, and I could always be the hero. I wore green army clothes and had a favorite plastic machine gun. I tied a string from the barrel to the stock, so I could slip it over my shoulder on long marches.

Eventually the trigger snapped off. After that, I made the noises with my mouth.

*

Finally, the brothers moved away. So, I played army by myself. I pretended they had been killed in action, and there was an elaborate death scene. I vowed revenge on the dreaded Germans, and in fact soon captured an entire battalion single-handedly.

At the awards ceremony, I pinned my medal to their caskets.

*

The scene of my great exploits was Mr. Patterson's big field. He was old, and once dated my great-aunt. They would ride in a horse and buggy down Main Street.

He let the kids play softball in his field. Once, a window was broken.

Years later, when I was older, I heard stories.

He was accused of touching a young neighbor girl. The girl and her family remained friends with him, though. So I considered the source of the story, and how the two never got along.

*

A new neighbor moved in next door. I met him one morning when he was trying to unscrew the top part of the fence. Finally, he got it off, and stuck a lit M-80 down there. He put the top piece back on and stuck a finger in each ear.

I did the same.

When the M-80 went off, it blew the top piece of the fence high into the air like a rocket.

*

Later, we wrestled in his back yard. He beat me each time, and laughed in my face. He said, "Now we know I can kick your ass any time I want."

As time went on, he threw a knife at a neighbor girl, pelted my dog's doghouse with a BB gun, and fought with the local police, putting one of them in the hospital.

He went to prison soon after his eighteenth birthday, where I hope he was damaged internally.

His brother became a lawyer, for the sole purpose of keeping his little brother out of trouble. The lawyer and I would play basketball together. I was pretty good back then.

*

The neighbor on the other side kept attack dogs. Once, I had seen them dismantle a rabbit in seconds. Only bits of fur were left. Their owner hung his arms over the fence, and was grinning. He said, "Keeps them out of the garden."

I thought, The dogs or the rabbits?

He would bring over fresh tomatoes and cucumbers from his garden. In later years, there was a grapevine, which he put up in honor of my mother the spring after she died. He'd taken a large flat stone, carved a saying, and laid it in the dirt.

He watched me grow up. His oldest daughter had a crush on me. She was a couple of years younger, and spent a lot of time trying to kiss me on the cheek. Once, we were playing in a fort he had made for her. He thought he saw my hand somewhere it had not been. He grabbed me by the arm and threw me over the fence.

I landed hard, and it started to rain. I stayed there a very long time.

When I went inside, I was covered in mud. My mother said, "Let me see your hands."

I held them out.

She said, "Now turn them over."

I did.

In my hands, she was looking for guilt. Then, she looked for it in my face. Eyeing me like a fish, she made a decision, and told me, "Go wash up for dinner."

It wasn't over, though.

The neighbor had his eye on me.

There were dirty looks and fingers pointed. There was foul language. Once when I was walking home from school, he tried to run me over with his truck. I had to leap into the bushes.

One day, grinning, he came up to the fence. He said he had a new engine he was working on. It was in the garage. Come on over and take a look.

I backed away.

When he let one of the dogs loose on me, my father had to go over there. He was gone a long time. I heard crashes, and general scuffling. When my father returned he went straight into the bathroom, my mother following behind him.

The next day my neighbor had a black eye.

If a childhood is a box to put things in, there is never enough room for all the battlefields.

*

Hiding

Once, I grew a beard that was thick and unruly. I thought I could hide behind it. I thought I could stand in a room of people I knew with absolutely no fear of being approached. When my aunt failed to recognize me, I knew my plan had worked.

Later, I found out she had Alzheimer's.

*

I do not like my face.

I do not like my body, which is why I wear loose clothes.

When I don't like myself at all, I stay inside my apartment for days at a time.

I have sat in the back row at school, and stood in the corners of bars. Often, I avoid eye contact with strangers in the street.

I am always hiding.

*

One time, as a child, some of the neighborhood kids were playing hide-n-seek. I was "it".

I pressed my palm to a tree, stuck my forehead to my knuckles, closed my eyes and counted a hundred.

I couldn't find the kids.

I looked under cars, in bushes, behind garbage cans. Finally I gave up and yelled, "Olly olly oxen free!"

No one appeared.

Later, I found out they had gone home.

*

Most likely it was here I acquired the idea that it was better to be lost than found. Somehow it seemed wiser to be the one looked for, than the one looking.

As in many areas, certain roles would reveal certain rewards. And punishments.

Trudging home, I felt foolish. But I had learned something.

*

In my backyard, as a kid, there was a hollowed-out tree trunk. The tree trunk was positioned in a way that allowed someone to crawl inside so their whole body fit.

Often I would lie in there when it rained, and not get wet. The sound of the rain would make me sleepy. I felt safe, and would dream.

*

Old Man Lohr walked up and down our street with his zipper down. The kids would run and hide until breathless.

We thought he would beat us with his cane, and then swallow us whole.

My parents laughed at the dinner table when I relayed the day's harrowing events. My father said, his smile curling, "He's just an old man."

The only time Old Man Lohr ever "caught" me, he scowled right in my face.

I shuddered.

He said, "Next time you fail a math test I will eat your eyeballs raw!"

That night, I never studied so hard in my life.

To tease me, my sister threw salt in my eyes, saying, "That's how Old Man Lohr likes them!"

*

Mrs. Lohr hated us too. Late one night she banged on the door, waking us all up. With the whole family crowded in the doorway, she ranted and raved. She claimed our cat had clawed his way through her porch screen, and "attacked" her precious Siamese.

It turned out to be a romantic endeavor, and soon there were tiny feline creatures everywhere, like puffs of cotton.

I remember her eyes being large and red, like a witch's. I remember spittle flying from her quivering lip. I remember the nasty snarl. I remember the sharp pointy teeth like fangs. I remember the harsh smell of her words, her "bad breath". I was very young.

But I remember hiding behind my mother's housecoat, and then later sleeping in my parent's bed because I was terrified.

*

After that, the front door of my house became my enemy. There were two small windows on the top, in a row.

I believed that at night these windows were eyes – Old Lady Lohr's eyes. Terrified, I would run through the room as fast as I could before the death rays would get me.

Peeking in from the other room, waiting for just the right moment, I would make my mad dash to safety. Once, when I tripped and fell, I started to cry.

*

Old Man Lohr died first. After that, his wife turned friendly, inviting us inside for cookies, giving us pennies.

She began to ride an old-lady bicycle. It had wide handle-bars, and a large clumsy basket in front. She could be seen in town, on Main Street, pedaling in from a past century. Often she would stop by the breakfast restaurant, holding onto the telephone pole, bonnet, silk scarf knotted at her throat, fresh-air cheeks red in a raw breeze, eyes glowing through their age, a happy healthy slightly eccentric smile for the world.

Then, she died too.

My mother said it was a shame, and used the word 'unique'.

*

When I had the beard, a friend's older sister touched my face. Rough to the touch, she brought her hand back quickly. "It's like barbed-wire," she said, frowning. "What are you afraid of?"

I told her, "Everything."

She said, "I've seen your face. I like it better without the beard. This is why you don't have a girlfriend. You're afraid to be yourself."

*

On the table, a bowl of fruit was rotting. The grapes would soon be raisins. The apples had bruises. The lone banana longed sadly for the bunch.

She asked about me. "What?" I said.

She said, "In life. What is your scheme, your plan? What are you up to?"

I told her, "My neck."

*

She said, "California is in your eyes. Last night you dreamed about San Francisco. You want to read books on the beach, and write about sadness. I don't think any of the girls in your life have ever given you what you need."

I am silent.

The floors are coy this time of year. They avoid my gaze. My cheeks flush slightly.

*

My friend came in the room and saw us on the couch together. He knew better and only said, "Let's go."

We were going to another friend's to play music in his garage. He carried a guitar case by the handle. His sister had picked up a book, and crossed her legs. Her scent hung in the air, gently pulling me in her direction. She called out, "What are you hiding from tonight?"

I told my friend to go without me.

*

Still
photography

When I was nineteen, I began to see myself differently. Suddenly, there was a space between the past and the present. It was something rigid. A slab of concrete that ran farther than the eye could see. A stone desert. Over night, while the cement was drying, some kids had grabbed a stick.

What they wrote was: We aren't stupid, you know.

I signed my name to it.

*

There was no going back now.

My childhood was over. The mark on that place on my body continues to serve as Exhibit A, the evidence of my desperation. The proof that, by nature, I am sad.

*

To illustrate this, one day I borrowed my sister's camera. I drove to the cemetery. My subjects were guaranteed to sit still. Since I knew they couldn't move, this gave me time to evaluate the scene – its time, its place.

My life follows a similar plot.

When things move too fast, there *is* no time. But when they are slower, that's when I realize.

*

My first snapshot was the headstone of a soldier who died in the Korean War. He was nineteen – about the age of my eye through the lens that day. About the age of my father when he was stationed in Panama.

Next, a headstone from the Viet Nam War. He was my age, too. His last name was famous in my town.

*

Hovering over a tiny headstone, the rain got in my eyes. Despite clear skies, I moved forward in my mind.

He was born the same year I was, the same month. The headstone read: *Born And Died February 1966.*

He would have been in my class? We would have been friends? I would have dated his sister?

All day I trudged the grounds with my camera, counting to a million. Later, when my sister got the film developed, she asked questions. The look on her face meant I might as well be alone in the world.

She didn't have the darkness.

She would never understand.

*

As kids, come autumn we raked leaves into big piles. One after the other we took turns running and diving into the soft protuberance.

One of the kids had a talent. He could do a somersault right before he landed.

One day, he did his somersault, and landed with his arms outstretched like a diver. He hit face first. Initially when he didn't move, we urged him on, called him names. With a hand on his knee, the next kid was raring to go. "Come on!"

Soon, though, we had to get his parents.

Someone had put a rock at the bottom of the leaves.

*

There was a girl on my street a year older. One Christmas she received a camera. That morning, when she knocked on my door, my mother smiled.

We were young.

It was a film camera, a movie camera. Her parents envisioned another Orson Welles. In the snow, we trudged into the woods, where she had already set the scene. She lashed me to a cross. It was clumsy and I had to lean against a tree.

She ran the camera.

In an announcer's voice, she enunciated clearly. She said, "My father says you are a dirty Italian, but he hates Jews more. This film is for you, daddy. There are two of us left. Noah was a pervert – trust me."

With the camera running against her eye, she snapped her fingers. Immediately, two younger girls clad in white robes took their positions. They cowered at the foot of the cross, each grabbing a leg and weeping. I could feel their breath against my crotch, and see it in the late-December air.

*

Another time, she assembled a whole cast in order to re-enact the Sharon Tate murders. There was fake blood everywhere. The leader wore a gorilla mask and the first girl killed had warts. Since the event took place outdoors, and there were no walls, several extras held large white placards.

All the original scrawled words appeared in graphic red drippy paint. You know the words.

*

Another time, she went to a butcher shop. She bought several hunks of meat, and dumped them in the road.

Someone held up a cardboard cut-out of the sun.

Someone else held up a cut-out American flag.

Several "actors" crawled around on their hands and knees. With confused looks, they attempted to fit the hunks of meat together.

Traffic stopped.

Out the window of a compact car, a man in a tie was the first to ask. One of the "actors" said, "We are trying to put the cow back."

*

Freshman year was full of children trying not to be their parents. My friend's Xmas film made the yearbook, and I was a small-time star.

All through high school, she carried her camera. No one was safe. Towards the end of our last year, she played her completed film. It was called "Four Years".

The school hierarchy refused her use of the auditorium. So she showed it outside against the brick wall. She showed it in machine shop. She showed it in the cafeteria. She showed it wherever she could.

In college, she dabbled in experimental film, which the university labeled as "porn".

By 25 I had returned from the West Coast. The new fresh air in my lungs made me feel lighter. In a coffee shop I told her, "There is something missing in my life." I was smoking then, a habit that lasted only briefly. I tapped out the ashes into a plastic tray. They fell over like old men.

She smiled, and brushed back my hair, revealing a fresh bump at the hair-line, next to an old one.

She said, "Something, or someone?"

*

Later that year, at the party of a mutual friend, we sat in a corner and talked. Over and over, she tucked her hair behind her ear. She smiled, "Remember when you were my Jesus?"

I said, "My mother thought it was cute."

Her smile faded. "I never meet any one interesting any more."

Realizing something, I said, "Where's your camera?" It may have been the only time I didn't see her with it.

She said, "What camera?"

Later, I found out she had sold it for weed. As she was leaving, she told me. Solemn, she whispered, "I'm the one who put the rock there."

*

Recently I came across a bunch of old boxes. Inside one were photographs, among them my cemetery subjects. Thinking about it now, I should have brought a shovel that day and interviewed them in person.

My first question, of course, being, "What is death?"

Brushing off the dirt, the dead baby would say, "What is life?"

*

My uncle the soldier is buried in the same cemetery as my mother. There is a ritual involved in such visits. I am a modern man, and choose my ghosts carefully.

My sister said, "I never go any more."

I said, "We are always going."

*

Voodoo
doll

A woman I have "known" returns with pins: one for each eye, one for each ear, and one for what rubs against the inside zipper of my pants.

Jane.

A thousand miles is one foot step. Next door is across the world.

Every night, she said she loved me. Whenever I said it back, she didn't understand why we weren't living together.

"The pins," I said quietly.

*

A jet-liner is an invention the Wright Brothers never imagined. These days, the speed it takes for a person to go from one place to another is disturbing.

Don't blink your eyes.

A graduation has taken place.

We are not the same nation we started out as. Everything happens too easily now, too quickly. There is no longer time to contemplate. Instead of deciding, things are decided for us.

So in what seemed like minutes, she arrived with holsters. In each holster was a loaded six-shooter. Each bullet had my name on it.

How I missed those pins!

A graduation has taken place.

We spent half our time walking on the beach, and the other half in the bedroom, rubbing our skin together to start fires. The paint melted and the windows nearly burst. The flames were in our throats.

I was pronouncing my name wrong all of a sudden. I was bumping into furniture. In the middle of the night, she would climb inside my head. She would sneak around. She would snoop.

What are you looking for!

You...

On the beach, we passed women in bikinis.

She said, "Society promotes this, and society is male dominated. All men are predators. They want my eighteen year old daughter because her skin is fresh and her boobs stick straight out. You're no different. Soon, you won't want me any more. You'll want a younger version. That's why you'll never meet my daughter."

Her daughter had been in college plays. She was fresh-faced, and energetic. She pouted and laughed. She kicked her leg high, and danced on her toes. She sang. Pictures had been sent. Unsure of how to respond, I was careful. If I said, "She's beautiful," I was doomed.

If I said, "Um, nice," I was damned.

What I appreciate, of course, is peace in my life. Luckily, I found the right words, and told her, "She looks very talented."

⋆

There was an incident upstairs, and the dog hid under the bed. The words made my head spin. And our bodies seemed to cut through the air.

I said, "You're crazy! You've just talked for two hours without taking a breath, and said absolutely nothing."

"Crazy is a power word men use to control women!"

When the glass "fell", exploding against the floor linoleum, we stared. Furious, I had to leave.

I went for a walk.

When I returned, my nephew was in the kitchen, cooking. His eyes were glassy and he smelled like smoke.

He was sitting on top of the tile counter. His lips moved in slow motion. "It all comes down to this. Either the dawn beats you, or you beat the dawn. Only one of you walks away." But, it wasn't light out yet, and Dawn was a girl I *used* to know.

"I can hear you at night," he said.

"It was a bad idea."

As if on cue she appeared in the archway, wearing a white slip and holding an unlit cigaret to her lips. In a hush, she addressed my nephew. "He thinks I knocked over that glass, but I think it was him."

I rolled my eyes.

The door closed behind her, and she was outside, smoking and casting evil spells. The moonlight remembered her, and was kind. I watched my nephew's pot boil over. He was grinning.

*

The next day, in a Chinese restaurant, she asked me to name the women I had known.

When I began, she got sad. By the time the waitress arrived with a difficult smile and an order pad, she was ready to cry.

"Don't ask me any more questions," I told her when the waitress was gone.

"You weren't supposed to answer them," she said, teary.

It was better, later in the day at the beach. She held my arm and we sifted toes through the sand. The sky was bare, and only a few sea gulls glided. The rest of them, I figured, were off somewhere looking for women of their own.

Everyone thinks it's better to be somebody else. Everyone thinks it's better to have a woman on your arm. As we strolled, I watched a kid with a surf-board. He was alone with the sea. His legs were long. He sprinted into the surf.

She said, "Let's sit."

She said, "I am finding out."

She said, "I don't expect you to marry me, but you will have to fuck me better than that if you expect me to keep up this charade."

*

The wind became heavy, and pressed our clothes to our bodies. The sun was high. She said, "I think I am always dreaming. I've had the idea for this kind of thing since I was little. I'm older now, and it never fits the dream."

"We were lied to as children. False images were projected."

"I get angry when it doesn't happen right."

"Listen, I understand your position, but you have to understand mine. We are standing across the world from each other."

"But I'm in your arms."

*

Two men fished off jetty rocks. Their poles were long, and the lines they cast seemed to go out forever.

We stopped, and one of them said, "Sir, your wife is a striking woman."

The other said, "Are those buck teeth? I wonder what that means at night."

I looked at him strangely, while she smiled with her mouth closed.

*

On the back deck, under the moon, we lazed on the soft wood planks. She smoked a cigaret. She said, "I came a thousand miles to watch you gawk at a bony waitress."

I said, "Her bones are the issue here?"

She said, "You only like movies where everybody dies in the end." She blew out the smoke. The dog next door whimpered. A chicken was loose.

*

In the taxi to the airport, she held my hand and didn't say a word. Inside the airport, about to get in line, I handed her the bag and tried to kiss her. She pulled away. "I get nauseous when people watch."

Suddenly the bag was too heavy, and she put it down.

*

Her eyes are often harsh. They softened when she told me she wouldn't date anybody else. There were tears. She said home would be too lonely. When am I coming back, she wanted to know. I don't know, I said, when are you coming back?

I remember thinking, "It would be really awful if the plane crashed." And then right after, thinking, "Would it really?"

Her flight was called and she went through the gate. I stood there until I couldn't see her. On the escalator, there was a pretty girl.

*

On the taxi ride home, I stared out the window, wondering what had just happened. The driver was suddenly talkative. "Your wife?" he wanted to know.

"No."

"Girlfriend?"

"Well..."

He stopped asking questions.

It was a long ride, and after a period of silence, he suggested a drink. We stopped at a bar where young women dance without their clothes. We ordered two scotches. The women showed us their chests.

Before long, I realized that when I gave one a dollar she would go away. Since I wanted them to go away, I used up my money fast.

"Now, this is living," the old driver said with his tongue hanging out.

*

The
emergency
sambuca

My mistake was making the keys. Before leaving for the airport, she left them on the table. I considered another set, a secret set, one she had made when I wasn't looking.

Such an act would fit one of her personalities.

I remember it simply. There was no knock on the door, no warning. The lock simply turned, the door opened, and before the full act of swinging the heavy door wide was completed, the flesh of her palm, traveling at nearly light-speed, had made impact with the flesh of my cheek. "You shit!"

I rubbed the sore skin. "You know in a way, I was expecting you."

Inside, she threw a bag across the living-room. It sailed past the stereo and knocked over a lamp. Suddenly, her finger was an inch from my nose. "No one blocks out my email address."

"You flew a thousand miles for this?" My eyes drooped. I was exhausted and there were pains in my chest.

"I drove!"

*

A little while later, she was in a chair, slightly calmer. I brought a glass cloudy with booze and handed it to her, which she refused. She made a face. "All you alcoholics are the same. You think a little bourbon solves everything." She sat with her arms folded.

"It's sambuca," I moaned.

I sipped from it.

Soon, there was a commotion outside. We ran to the balcony, which overlooked the parking lot. Two cars had collided. Steam was coming out of a crumpled hood. Three figures stood in a small circle, their faces variously distorted.

The words were loud. There was talk of the weather. As in, "Whether or not you know it, this was your fault."

And, "Whether the sun shines or it rains like cats and dogs, we are alive to see it."

And, "I'm calling the cops whether you like it or not."

Like a pistol, a cell-phone is drawn from a purse. The weapon is aimed, and numbers are dialed, while his hands are held out in a begging gesture.

*

When we got downstairs, the woman was talking on the phone. The man was pleading with her. He was older, and didn't speak English very well. He said, "Please. Only in country to see daw-ter. Rented car."

She gave him a quick head to toe, and a small sneer. "I'm tired of fighting your war," she said.

*

Giving up, the man walked over to the woman's passenger. She was younger, pregnant, and rested sideways on a curb with her legs straight out. He administered to a small cut above her eye. She was gentle with him, allowing it.

Jane stared angrily.

*

Off the phone now, the woman had a triumphant look. She saw us, and said excitedly, "What did you see!"

I told her, "I think I saw you fall in love once."

Jane said, "I saw the bloom come off my own rose."

We walked back upstairs, very sad.

*

She unpacked her bag, pulling a sweater out first, and then a soft-cover book. It was the book we did together. First my poem, then one of hers, then one of mine, then hers, until mercifully it ended.

She had been very excited when it first came out. They are love poems. My friends crucified me, and I had to hang there and take it. A little while later, with tea, I was sitting in a chair flipping through it. She said. "At first

I thought you didn't like me. I mean, I didn't know. You wouldn't touch me for a long time, but when you did things were different. The feeling was strong."

I told her, "It's because I take my time with women. I was raised by four of them. I don't always know what they want. Also, I'm shy, and embarrassed of my body. I go slow, in order to be sure."

"Why do you always have to be sure?"

*

She fidgeted. It was her craw, and what was stuck. She said, "You keep women down by making them think you don't care."

"It's not on purpose. I told you."

"This is how you control them. By making your face sympathetic, but hiding your real self behind it. You are devious, because you make adjustments to your personality as you go along. You're trying to fool me. And then I don't know how to react to you."

She was staring, boring dreamy holes into the ceiling tiles. She was depositing herself into the crevices. She was fighting herself by fighting me. She was pretending to be honest. She pulled on her lower lip, and said, "You are trying to be confusing. It's a strategy. Men are well known as soldiers. You want a war, but you don't want to start it. I think there is a psychological term for that."

"You make me tired," I told her.

"Passive aggressive," she said.

*

I informed her she was the one who liked to fight. She couldn't be happy when things were peaceful. In order to feel anything, she needed the drama. She asked if I was feeling warm, if I had a fever.

She made a face.

I was speaking a foreign language. Making outrageous claims.

But, for proof of my theory, the argument arrived on time. She began with, "It's a good thing you don't have a cat. I would have killed it by now."

I said, "I know what nasty is. I grew up with it."

"Your friends are appalling. Their jokes are low-grade, and even the women curse, if you can call them women."

"At least I have friends."

But, this wasn't the argument. No, listen outside, through the window, for that engine just starting to warm.

*

Picking her teeth from a fresh kill, she said, "I won't have sex with you again until you see a doctor."

"Stop it," I said.

She said, "The last time I was here, I noticed a cluster of warts on your genitalia, something I hadn't noticed on the visit before. Are you fucking poor girls again?"

She stared at the wall, at a photograph in a frame. Inside, my nephew had his arm around me. We were grinning. On purpose, she scanned the walls instead of my face. She said to a new picture, "That's what you get for messing with girls who didn't go to college."

I didn't go to college, I remind her. And she said, "I miss your beautiful soul. What happened to the boy who woke every day with the sunlight?"

"He met you," I said, dryly.

*

Suddenly, I was worried. "You saw warts down there *last* visit, and you're only telling me *now*?"

I thought, Maybe I *should* see a doctor. My doctor is a woman, and she judges me. She scowls when my weight is too high. She frowns when I tell her the truth about how much I drink.

My doctor asks about my job, and I avoid the subject. She thinks I should quit, because it is stressful. She has said, "You know, a man your age, at your weight – stress will kill you before a car accident."

Now *warts*, I must show her? She has yet to see me with my pants down.

To Jane, I said, "Why are you here?"

*

Her father was a bear of a man, big and bearded, a motorcycle at his crotch. A poet. She once said, "I write because he wrote. He scribbled on the walls, and now so do I."

Often, he was in trouble with the law, and spent many nights in the backs of police cars, and many more in empty local cells. It was the restlessness. It was his own mind working against him.

Eventually, the State came with a deal. All for a bed, meals, care, comfort, stability, and enough bars to keep him in one place for a while, he merely had to give up the beautiful part of himself.

Schizophrenia is a gene, passed down, like male pattern baldness, like gas. It runs in families. She climbs in my lap, and puts her ear to my heart.

"You should go home," I said.

"I'm not him," I said.

She informed me, "Your mother is still dead. I will bring it up only as a last resort, only when you bring up my father, and only in a way that no one else would ever view as cruel. But, you and I both know what's going on here."

I said, "I'm glad I don't have a cat."

"I have been touched by the good intentions of Jesus. I intimidate you. You are afraid of my good moral character."

I said, "You buy dishes at yard-sales just so you'll have something to break when you get mad."

"That was a long time ago!"

"You're mad now..."

"Ohhhh!"

Morosely, I told her the dishes were in the top cabinet, and walked out of the room.

*

In the morning, we would find an actual rooster in the hallway, and a box of old clothes. She walked over to my books, which were piled in the corner. She ran her finger along them from top to bottom, and then repeated the process from bottom to top. She sucked on the finger. "Those are just the ones I read last year," I said.

She twisted the finger around a naughty smile.

I sniffled. "I'm ugly without them. It's the words that are the pretty part."

"I want your body."

"You love me because I remind you of your father. I'm the closest you can ever get to..."

She held up a hand. She swallowed hard. "If you bring up Freud, I will absolutely never speak to you again."

She was drooping, a sad flower in a corner. "So, what are we doing."

I said, "Tell me you'll stop censoring me. Tell me I can talk to you, whatever it is. Tell me the jealousy will stop, the temper tantrums. Tell me you're never going to dump your childhood shit all over me again. Tell me we can finally sweep up all these egg-shells. If you can't, well, then there it is."

*

~

'It's better than having
a dirty face...'

West coast

Halfway between twenty and thirty, I solidified an earlier decision. By selling my electric guitar to a man in an alley, I was seeking out another option. I was fulfilling the promise of the bible, the one written by Jean-Louis. Later, I would trade paper for paper and that night slept with a train ticket under my pillow.

A friend had an uncle on the west coast. The uncle had a small sailboat, where he lived instead of an apartment or a house with a yard. His yard was the Pacific Ocean.

It took three days to get there.

My father said, "*Where* are you going?"

*

She was a train attendant. She helped people with their seats and answered questions. She was our age. She said, "I live in Seattle. It's boring. I figured this job was a good way to see the country. My mother thinks I'm wasting my life. She sits in a chair all day and watches television. But *I'm* wasting my life."

I said, "I like the way your hair falls across your face. You're mysterious, and now I feel mysterious, too."

She said, "It's frizzy. Most days, I just feel ugly."

"You write, don't you?"

She said, "There are boys like you where I live."

*

In the train lounge, the bartender was drunk. In the middle of announcing drink specials over the intercom system, he would break into song. Love songs. He mentioned girls by name.

When one would blush, she would stand out, and we knew.

I brought my book, and sat at a table. Leo said, "You can't have the whole cake. Daddy just gives crumbs."

His eyes were crossed, and glassed over. His voice was deep, because he'd been born at the bottom of a pit and had to crawl up his whole life. He had a soul-patch, with tiny bits of gray.

After my third one I told him he was Batman. In return, he said he was too black to be Batman. All the superheroes are white. But he said he used to be a singer back when it meant something to be blue.

He pulled up his sleeve and showed me a mark. The skin was rippled, and had healed awkwardly. It was a bullet hole.

He mentioned a liquor store robbery, and being in the wrong place at the wrong time. He said, "Prison isn't what you see in the movies." He stopped talking.

I was learning about America. I was putting the pieces together. My small town was a coloring book, and all the crayons were black and white. I was coloring outside the lines now. I was drawing new pictures. I was allowed, because I allowed it.

The lounge was crowded.

A minor incident occurred, where I was accused of cutting in line. Somehow, I looked foolish, despite being in the right. Often, I have trouble presenting an accurate picture of myself.

This is my history. The maps run in circles, while the treasure is buried deep.

I hadn't seen my friend in a day and a half. By the time we got to Washington, we were no longer talking.

*

My friend's uncle stuck out a hand. He reminded me of Jimmy Buffet. He took us to Seattle in his car. The car rattled and the radio played static, until the weather report, which was as clear as the skies that day.

Outside one bar, about to go in, a guy was sleeping against a lamp post. His hair seemed clamped to his forehead. His eyes wouldn't open. I dislike the word "homeless" when it is a category.

I traded him my shoes for his.

Inside the bar, my friend's uncle introduced us around. He bought us beers, and also burgers that instead of an onion had a slice of pineapple.

He slapped his nephew on the back and said, "It's about time you came to your senses!"

*

One of his uncle's friends wiped his mouth with a sleeve. He made a face and said, "I like your shoes."

I told him, "I am re-living my past life. I remember you. You were the stable boy, and I was the horse."

He slapped me on the back. We drank shots.

*

Later, we drove in my friend's uncle's car down the pier. The pier was old wood and narrow. It creaked and we drove slowly. There were small fishing boats docked on both sides, and men standing around with their hats pushed up on their foreheads. Some of them coiled rope. Some of them filled water tanks. We stopped finally, and got out.

He introduced us to his friends.

One said, looking me and my friend over, "This skinny one's your nephew? I thought it was the other one."

I am pudgy, and so was my friend's uncle.

There are many ways of calling someone fat.

*

That evening, we drove to his uncle's small town. At the marina, my friend disappeared for the toilet. His uncle and I took a rowboat to the sailboat, which was anchored. I remember the rowboat nearly at the same level as the water, and a little of the water seeping in.

That night, we slept like giants.

The boat rocked, and the moon was full, and I was very far from home. At dawn, I wrote postcards.

*

Later, one of them said, "Look."

It was the sky, the distance. It was the colors, and the plain view of home. It was mountains, and fresh air. My lungs felt new. My heart was clean. I breathed.

I looked.

*

Towards noon, we went shopping for provisions. In the grocery store, a mile-long aisle contained nothing but beer. Mostly with names I had never heard of. My friend's uncle said it was because of all the micro breweries in the area. Anybody and their mother, he said, could start their own beer brand.

And most of them did.

At the checkout, with a full cart, my friend's uncle pulled out a credit-card and paid for everything. He knew somebody in line. They shook hands.

"I'm real sorry how everything turned out."

"So'm I."

"I tried to call."

"Yeah."

"It's not her fault. Blame me."

The guy's eyes were down. His hands were in his pockets. His foot moved in slow circles.

*

We motored out into The Puget Sound. In the sunshine, my friend and I held beer bottles. Our feet were up. My friend's uncle was steering, sun-glasses, and small sailor's cap. Suddenly, he was leaning out the back with his penis out, "watering the sharks".

He mentioned "pirates".

Later, he said, "If any Coast Guard boats come up, I do the talking." He emphasized the word 'I'.

Live prawns crawled around in the little fridge. They had gotten out of the bag. When I reached in, one crawled up my arm. I jumped.

My friend's uncle said, "If you're squeamish now, just wait." He was smiling. Later, on an island, there would be ten-inch slugs. There would be spiders big as my fist. My friend would grab a slug. He'd hold it up like a prize fish. He'd chase me with it.

Soon, his uncle cut the engine. In a matter of minutes, he taught us the basics of a sailboat, and we were a working crew. I was learning knots. One day, I hope to untie myself.

When we pulled on certain ropes, the sails rose like eagles. Their wing-span made my head spin. The bow of the sailboat cut through the waves, and we glided.

When we pulled on other ropes, the weight shifted. We slowed, and there was time for things to sink in.

In the water there was a splashing.

I wanted it to be baby whales, or dolphins. When they were otters, I watched their heads puncture through the surface. They twisted around each other at maniacal speeds. They dove down underneath for several minutes, churning the water, before bobbing back up.

They repeated this. They played.

His uncle became excited. He thrust his finger. "Look!" he said. "Born performers! The sea! The sea!"

My friend's uncle squinted and pointed all the way up. At the top of the mast was a small basket. He poked his nephew in the chest. He said, "You're the skinny one. That's the crow's nest. In a little while, you'll climb up and be a lookout."

My friend looked ashen.

His uncle slapped him on the back.

My friend sighed in relief.

*

In Friday Harbor, a port town, we steered the boat into a space in the marina. It was like parking a car. At the last minute I forgot all my knots, and my friend's uncle had to tie them or we would crash.

In town, at a restaurant, my friend's uncle lifted his beer glass. There was food in his mouth. He said, "Today you were sailors! Tomorrow who knows!"

Excitedly, I babbled about earlier in the day, when my friend and I were jumping around tying knots, wrapping and unwrapping rope, shifting sails and maneuvering the traveler. How at one point the front sail got caught. How I jumped up after it, running the deck like an obstacle course.

We could feel the muscles in our arms.

We could feel our brains cinching around certain new ideas.

My friend's uncle's eyes twinkled. "Listen. You'll never know what you can do unless you push yourself." He brought the beer mug down hard on the table, so some of the beer splashed out. "If you don't push, you don't know."

In the restaurant, my friend disappeared. He threw out his chair, and left. Imagine a cat sprinting out of the room for no reason.

His uncle leaned in. He said, "Is that one alright?"

"Yeah. He's just fine."

*

A waitress sat down. Her face was hard but her eyes were soft. They spoke warmly to each other, exchanging looks. Suggestions were made, and one of them blushed. Finally, her hand was on his cheek.

"You going to help me with my homework later?"

When she was gone, he sat back, allowing himself to breathe. "About to graduate college, that one. Forty three years old, two boys at home."

"She's pretty."

"Yeah, there's that."

*

The cook, at his post, could be seen through a cut-out in the wall. He yelled out television trivia questions as he flipped shrimp and tossed vegetables. The steam shot up into his face. I liked his hat.

When the question came to "Happy Days", I shouted the answer, which was a tough one. People looked. Later, the cook would remember me.

*

First, we staggered down the road. Then, we pushed through a door. We sat in a bar. Our table was high and crooked and required three matchbooks to even things out. My friend's uncle asked for quarters, and then played Bob Marley songs on the jukebox.

The cook came in, and sat at our table. I offered my Yankee cap in exchange for his fedora. He declined. I went to the bathroom.

When I returned, "ghosts" were the topic.

My friend's uncle said, "I swear there was no one at the wheel, but it kept turning anyway. By midnight, we were halfway there – right on course! You tell me."

The cook said, "My girlfriend talks to her mother." He emphasized the word "talks". Continuing, he said, "I am not a man afraid of the unknown. My parents are Santería, so voodoo was in my house when I was a kid. But one night her mother spoke to me, through her daughter. Yeah, it was weird."

My friend's uncle said, "Well, what did she say?"

"She said don't eat meat and stop looking at underage girls."

*

In the morning, we left Friday Harbor. The chill was in my bones, and when I breathed I could see it in small white clouds.

Sailing again, we came upon a grouping of islands. At the small dock, my friend's uncle instructed my friend and me to jump out. From the boat he threw us ropes, and told us to wrap them around the poles.

He said, "Hold on tight until I tell you not to."

It turned out that if we lost the ropes before all was secured, the boat would drift into the bay, and 'somebody' would have to swim out after it.

*

Briefly,
Amsterdam

In Amsterdam every cafe has tables outside.

Slowing down is a way of life. With sunglasses up over my head, I sit in the sunshine writing in a sketch-pad, "The women here are blonde and they smile."

"They all ride bikes and their breasts bounce."

"They are free and easy here."

"America is too tense. I see it now."

My friend, a married woman with anger issues, sat sipping a drink and blinking in the sunshine. My nephew talked to a man at the curb about a motorcycle. Soon, my nephew was riding on the back of it, roaring down the street, his hands waving in the air.

The grease in his hair kept it in place. His cool American flower-shirt billowed as they rounded the block and disappeared.

It was true my love for America was jaded. I had seen drab skies, and watched the faces of people fall in the street. I had seen too much. Soon, I found out the sky in Europe was the same as the sky in New York. Only I can change.

Revelations approach me gently.

It's the people who rub me the wrong way.

When we landed, the youngest in our group, my nephew, said, "Is it real?"

*

Our hotel was three flights up, steep and narrow. Giddy, we dragged our bags skyward at different paces. My nephew, in his twenties, was far ahead. Mired on the second floor was myself. Bringing up the rear, one floor below, was my married friend.

We reported our struggles, at various points, gleeful like children, shouting out our progress. Later, in my notepad, I would write, "I shouldn't die yet, it's just beginning."

The room itself was on the corner of the building. Two large bay windows made the act of waking up a sensual encounter. Each morning, my nephew stuck his head out the window that overlooked the canal, and yelled, "Good morning, Amsterdam!"

If there were boats going by, the people would wave up and yell back.

*

I remember waking up with my leg out a window, and hearing in my half-dream state several different languages at once. They drifted along the sidewalk down below. Its music lulled me in and out of sleep.

*

Our first day, while my married friend slept, my nephew and I went downstairs. In the street, the sunshine was bright and warm. In a small bar, we asked for a menu. We ordered hash and smoked it quickly, as if the police would bust in.

The bartender grinned, and poured two beers.

"Americans," he must have been thinking.

*

In the street again, I said, "I love my feet."

We walked into many shops, bought a few postcards, a keychain. In another bar, the fourteen year old behind the counter gave us a sullen hello. Soon I would decide he wasn't sullen at all. He was 'cool'.

The beer was fresh and soothed my throat. My nephew asked about the women. He said, "Are they all blonde?"

The bartender smiled, and said, "I wouldn't know about that."

And so, without him knowing, I exchanged the word 'cool' for 'shy'. It was like sliding a dollar bill out of his pocket, or sliding one in.

I said, "Is it expensive to live here?"

His eyes widened.

*

He spoke numerous languages. "It's what I pick up by working here. There's people who live here, and there's everybody else."

He had no interest in America.

He was learning to count. When he ran out of fingers, he told us about his mother, who sold flowers in the square. "She makes my clothes," he said. "She made this shirt."

*

The Red Light District is cobble-stoned. When the moonlight touches down, the water in the canals splay off into patterns, and the canal is suddenly filled with diamonds. You can cup your hand, and lean over, or leave them. On walks, it is hard to imagine Nazis with machine guns patrolling such beauty.

I see a girl who looks like Ann Frank. Her lips are twisted. She's planning a wedding. She's looking for him.

I turn to my married friend. "Where's my nephew?"

She said, her eyes rolling, "This is good shit."

Later, we found him outside a bar. He was talking to two girls from Boston. His cheek was cut. "The motorcycle?" I said.

He breathed.

One of the girls leaned over me, and said, "You look angry."

I told her, "People always say that. Inside, I am smiling."

We took a walk, and only twenty paces in she hugged me. She said, "I have known you forever."

We walked down an alley.

A door opened and Jamaican music poured out. A kid stumbled down the street, trying for several minutes to light a cigaret. His hair was dreadlocked and bundled up in a hat, so he looked like a giant colorful lightbulb.

A little later, as I tried to re-trace certain steps, a girl in a doorway reached out a hand. They are not allowed to leave their window. I stayed just out of reach. Her fingers grasped the air in a smooth rolling motion. Her smooth black eyes were all business.

*

A
mystery

I live on the third floor. Across the parking-lot is one of those long cattle-car houses, narrow like a train. It's a summer rental, and is empty in the winter – usually.

One day, while I sat on my rotting balcony, I saw a hand in the window. The hand groped toward the shade. After several attempts, finally the hand pulled down the shade.

There was no car parked in front.

*

Later, during the night, I heard noises – three crashes and then a humming. The humming sustained itself for several minutes, and then halted abruptly.

I went back to sleep.

*

A few days later, my buzzer rang. The voice claimed to be the mailman.

I said, "You don't sound like my mailman."

The voice said, "The regular guy's off today."

The voice said it had a package for someone on the second floor. He said he rang their buzzer but no one answered. The voice said, "Can you buzz me in so I can leave it at their door?"

When I went down, the hallway was empty.

*

That night, I heard engines gunning. I went to the window, but saw nothing. In the morning, when I asked neighbors, each one said, "What engines?"

*

At times, my mind reels. I start thinking too much and come up with preposterous assumptions. For instance, when I have a fever I think it's the Bird Flu. When there is a ripple on my skin, it's Ebola. If my tooth hurts, I have cancer of the jaw.

My stomach gurgling is an ulcer.

My sore knee is a wheelchair in my future.

My stiff neck is a spinal injury.

Grogginess means Alzheimer's.

Gas is a heart attack.

A bloody nose is a brain tumor.

You get the idea. You could say I jump to conclusions.

*

At some point it is in my best interest to forget about the hand on the shade. Forget about the humming and the "mailman", and the engines.

I decided to concentrate on what was real.

I dialed the telephone.

On the other end, she said, "It's been a long time."

She said, "You used to be artistic and now you're just starved for attention."

*

I wanted to draw a picture called "The Fat Anorexic". With a black felt pen I made lines on thick paper. I curved some of the lines in order to create facial features.

I made breasts and buttocks and put pimples on her face. I placed a hand on her hip, and made her knee bend slightly.

I made her hair greasy somehow or at least in disarray. The expression on her face revealed disgust.

Finished, the scene was a bathroom. A slightly overweight girl in her twenties stared grudgingly at the toilet. The seat was up.

The caption read, "I hate throwing up."

On the phone, I wanted to tell her about it. I didn't.

Instead I said, "You still draw?"

She said back pointedly, "I only draw conclusions now."

Later when I thought about it, I realized the entire picture was made up of lines. All my drawings are the same: bare.

Minimal.

The people are stick figures. They are barely there.

This is also how I write.

This is also how I live.

This is also how I maintain relationships with women.

⋆

Her conclusions about me felt heavy. I had slipped into an iron overcoat. She held out the sleeves. With each step I sunk into the ground.

When she was finished talking, I was up to my waist.

"You never had any ambition," she accused.

She said, "At one point I wanted you to get me pregnant."

"We picked out baby names," I remembered.

⋆

The women in my life, she said. Are too tall. They look down on you. The worst part is you let them. She said, Oh God you haven't changed. "You still live inside your own head too much. You disregard everything real and opt for your own little world."

I said, "What's real?"

⋆

In a river once I lost my clothes. I was young, and refused to come out until a blanket was produced. The blanket had thorns in it and pricked me until there was blood.

It had been the picnic blanket.

There was also mayonnaise in my hair.

I shivered in the car while my father ran the heat. He laughed and messed my hair with his big plump hand. He smiled, so big that I remember it.

Years later he would wonder why I don't have a son. He couldn't understand it. I couldn't either. It was a mystery.

At the dumpster, I hefted over a bag of garbage. I saw a bag already in and noticed bones ripped through the plastic. The bones were too big for a chicken.

The wind whistled, and I thought I saw shadows.

Quickly, I twirled around.

When I turned back, I realized the "bones" were only old clothes hangers.

I had dialed her number from memory. She said, "When my mother died, you never called."

I told her, "I guess I've been thinking about you. Remember *afternoon delight*? Remember breaking the bed? Remember in the car, and the cop with the flashlight, and that stupid old maid neighbor?"

Impatient, she said, "We were young."

She told me she had been walking down the railroad tracks behind her house. She said it had snowed. She said she saw a man scurry into the woods. When she went over, there were only deer tracks.

That evening, she heard scratching at the window. When her husband got home, he went outside with a shotgun. Back inside, he removed his coat. "Nothing," he said.

In the morning, there was a knock on their door. A newspaper was left. On the front-page was a photograph. The photograph depicted a horrible train wreck. She said, "At first I misread the date. I thought the paper had last week's date on it. But then I looked closer."

Continuing, she said, "The strange thing was that Bill was supposed to be on that train. He had a meeting with his brother. Their father was sick. But he stayed with me because of the man I saw. What do you think it means?"

"You mean the man you didn't see?"

"Yes."

I said, "I often get chills at moments like these."

I thought I should try drawing again, to get my mind off things. I let the pen decide. Soon, there was a hand – bony and sharp-knuckled. The hand was pulling down a shade. On the roof, on his belly, was a dark figure – a spy. The spy reached down and grabbed the hand, locking in on the wrist bone.

The fingers of the hand abruptly straightened.

You can draw music if you try, and make it dramatic if you concentrate.

You can draw a shudder.

Later, when I was alone in a room, I drew a house with a chimney. It was a simple box house, with a V roof. Smoke came out of the chimney, and there was one door. This means only one way in and one way out.

It's no mystery that way.

★

Trumpet

At nearly 2am, I took my trumpet down to the ocean, slung down against my leg like a weapon. I live across the street. A last minute decision leaves my drink on the stove. I only have so many hands.

The sand is wet, and I sink in with my K-Mart sandals. Winter is a ghost tonight, as temperatures are high, and November has nothing to say for itself.

At the mouth of the water I shriek out a few fast notes, quick jabs at the night. The ocean jabs back, and then roars. Soon, I realize I can't keep up. I can't play with the master.

*

There are soft padded noises – footsteps. Next, I feel a sharp pain against the back of my neck. I fall to one knee, but don't go out. They try to take the horn, and then pull at my pockets.

I swing blindly with the horn, make vicious slashes at the air, before feeling something grab at my ankle. Teeth sink in at the bone. I feel nauseous. I fall to the sand. Fingers crawl across the back of my neck.

In the morning I examined the bite marks and determined they were human. I would most likely need a rabies shot.

*

The next night a friend and I went down there, to wait for them. He was angry, and paced. No one came around. We waited an hour. Finally, in the sand, he said, "My mother won't talk to me. She told me to drop dead. It's the alcohol. I told her I'm tired of pleasing everyone but myself."

"Jane's coming," I said. "I couldn't stop her." The ocean made a thick sound, a clap of thunder, a book coming down heavy on a table, the thud and thump of one wave pounding down on top of another.

I considered changing the locks, or changing my name. I considered claiming I wasn't me. Is it so implausible? Haven't you ever woken up as someone else?

Then I remembered something a friend always said when he had to deal with his ex-wife, "Handle your business. Be a man."

My friend mentioned Viet Nam, about getting lost in the street markets, and even working in the rice fields for pennies. I told him they didn't have pennies.

"They have rice fields, though, right?"

I said, "Yes. And Americans still in cages."

He said, "*This* is a cage."

*

At my job, there is a woman there I despise. She walked up and felt my head. "There's a bump," she frowned.

Later when I wasn't looking she tried to rub the side of her head against the side of mine. Jo Jo sidled up to me, the words drifting out of the side of her mouth like cartoon bubbles, "Guess who wants to get in your pants again?"

"Stop enjoying this," I said morosely.

*

"I heard you play the trumpet," another friend said, mocking me. Then, pretending to be this workplace admirer of mine, continued with, "Maybe we can get together. I've been known to play a pretty mean organ."

*

My admirer shows up again, a button missing. She said, "I heard you take your trumpet down to the ocean at night. I heard you play it when no one's around to listen."

I said, "Something like that."

"Maybe I'm dumb," she said, "but I could make us something to eat, and we could go down there together. You could play the trumpet, and then we could just sit there and listen to the sound the sun makes when it's going down."

"I might be crazy," I warned her.

"Oh, yeah. I've heard that."

"There's another woman," I said, finally. "Besides – didn't you used to be a man?"

Later, I remembered that was somebody else I was thinking of, and I felt bad.

*

My friend called from a payphone. He was in jail again. He got drunk and broke into her house, to see his son.

The child wasn't home, which made him frenzied. Contextually, the broken lamps and smashed-in television made sense.

In the morning I took the horn to a hock shop one town over. They would only give me a hundred and fifty for it. So, I sold my shoes, as well as the pants I had on. The belt buckle was a gift, and worth thirty dollars all by itself.

At the jailhouse, my friend was sober. His face hung through the bars. He was smoking a cigaret and talking to one of the guards.

The desk officer asked if I was his brother. I said, "Okay."

"You two don't look alike," he said.

"Different fathers," I didn't grin.

On the car ride home we saw a dog with three legs, and then a man on crutches. They both stopped when the light turned green, and went along their way when it turned red again.

*

Illness

He tugged at the tube up his nose, because it itched. He said, "When I was stationed in Panama my best buddy was Fischer. Fish was a Jew who spent money like a Dago and drank like a Mick. That's why we called him 'Fish' – because he drank like one."

Continuing, he said, "He was my best friend in Panama. When Fish had your back, he *had* your *back*. No worries. I saw him a few times after the war, but the wives didn't get along. His was a glamour girl, and your mother wanted a family."

⋆

We didn't always talk. Some days the television was enough, the ball-game, and the volume loud, and the heat too high. At times, words are not necessary, and so now you see the source of my affection for them.

They know their place.

It works this way with people, too.

I said, "You look tired."

My father said, "I'm always tired." When he smiled, I saw myself.

⋆

Fridays meant chemo. That's when they would pump his body with poison to kill other poison. It is hard to figure.

The treatments were in New York City, an hour and a half drive, depending on traffic. Once it took almost four hours, and we were late. In the parking garage there was a problem, and my brother-in-law took a swing.

The attendant apologized, and later they shook hands.

Since he had part of his pancreas removed, my father's blood-sugar became an issue. Diabetes set in. Each morning, afternoon, and evening, my sister would come in with a small machine.

My father would hold out his finger and turn his head. Smiling, he said, "Alright, Dracula."

She drew blood and then tested it on the machine. A number popped up on the little screen. They kept records in a notebook.

*

My father would push his good whiskey on me. There were bottles and bottles under the cabinet, next to the dog food. "Take it home," he would say. "I'll never drink it now."

His eyes would be bright, and he would smack his lips. He missed it. He missed the two fingers in a glass after work. He missed the beers with the boys at the VFW hall. "Well, I'm glad none of you kids smoke. That's one thing I was always glad for."

He said, "How's the car running?"

"Purrs like a kitten, Dad."

"Don't lie to me."

"Okay, it's a tough little car. It's hanging in there and so am I."

"If you need money..."

"I'll come to you if I do. I promise."

He said, "You still seeing that crazy one. What's her name?"

I said, "I see her sometimes."

He said, "This *sometimes*. Is this what you guys today call a relationship?"

My hands were in my pockets. I pawed at the carpet with a foot. "Yeah, pretty much, Dad."

Some days, his oxygen tubes were too tight, and they left long marks on his face. He would trace them a moment, before letting them go on without him.

Rocking back in his chair, he'd ask about the new Mets trade. When I told him, we shook our heads. Nothing makes sense. Laughing helps.

An alarm went off. He hit a button on the back of a small wind-up clock, and the ringing stopped. There was a tray-table with an array of pills laid out. He picked out a green one.

*

Uncles

I had an uncle who for many years lived very quietly by himself. Somewhere in the city, he rented a room in a boarding house. He cooked on a hot-plate. He bathed, and evacuated his bowels and bladder in a bathroom everyone on the floor shared.

He played a small wood guitar and collected dirty magazines.

He had a tiny refrigerator, inside of which he kept tiny bundles of food.

These would sustain him for 58 years.

⋆

At the holidays every year, my father would pick him up in our old blue station wagon. My uncle didn't drive. And bring him to our house.

I remember the car rides.

Some years we drove through the Sixties. Too young for that I only "remember" it from stories and photographs. In those photographs my father and uncle had long thick sideburns. They grinned innocently. Their stories were small dreams I attempted to decipher at a relative pace.

Some years we drove through the Seventies. I saw the colorful clothes and bad facial hair for myself. I remember Jimmy Carter and funny looking cars waiting in long gas lines.

I remember the Bicentennial.

I remember the blind-folded men in rumpled suits every day on the news.

There was only one year in the Eighties, the year he got sick. By the end of 1981, the blue station wagon car rides into the city were over.

⋆

At fourteen, I was unsure of myself. I had recently gotten a gold chain as a gift. I asked my uncle to help with the clasp. He was all thumbs though and was no help.

Then we played darts that had Velcro tips. Our relationship had changed. I didn't have as much time for him. He no longer amazed me. I had other amazing things in my young life.

Girls to impress.

Sports to star in.

Beers to drink behind the water tower on school nights.

*

In the living room, in a chair in the back, my uncle would tap his foot. It was a habit, as subconscious as it was loud and steady.

The family watched television.

Thud, thud, thud, went my uncle's foot on the floor. Thud, thud, thud. Finally, my father had to say something.

My father blurted, "Walt! I'll cut that goddamn foot off!"

Before the year was out, the doctors would do exactly that.

Cancer is a dirty word in my house.

*

He had been keeping time with that foot, like a metronome. A secret rhythm plugged into a secret universe. Music only he could hear. There was something in my uncle's head that fed him riches.

Mostly he kept his shiny pennies to himself. A collection of years and experiences, kind acts and wise words. But at times he would dump a handful in my lap, and his attention was a goldmine. He let me win at cards, but not all the time.

Years later, from his example, I let my own nephews win. But, not all the time.

It's better that way, when there's mystery, when there are two outs in the ninth inning and it could go either way. Sometimes you have to lose, in order to win. I wanted my nephews to understand the beautiful parts of failing. I thought this might be important.

*

When he was twelve, I sat down my sister's oldest child. From now on, I told him, you can say anything to me.

I figured on secrets, the things he would never tell his parents. With this inside information, I had hoped to keep him out of trouble.

Instead, he mistook 'say anything' for the freedom to curse wildly at me.

All in all, it worked out.

Under my watch, he was never arrested, didn't bounce from woman to woman, and was not once found naked and drunk in a public place while a baby Doberman licked his scrotum.

All that happened later.

*

At my uncle's funeral, forty folding chairs were set up. Only seven were used. His landlord from the city arrived late. She brought a check for the flowers, but had to borrow a pen.

Someone spoke. He was connected to the funeral home, and his suit was neat and crisp. He was solemn. "Walter was a Marine in World War Two. He fought on Iwa Jima. He was also a champion bowler, as his many trophies..."

My mother's two best friends were there. At some point I went up to them. I said something like, "Thank you for coming. I know it means a lot to my mother that you're here. My uncle was a very good man."

Days later, at the dinner table, my mother commented. She told us her friends mentioned how each of the kids had approached them. My mother was proud of that. She had always wanted to raise her children right.

It was her dream.

*

Garden
lady

Helen was eighty. She invited me in to see her plants. They winded themselves all around her home, several different kinds and colors. There were plants in the kitchen, the bedroom, the hallway, and the back room, soaking in the generous exposure.

At times, I could hear them snickering.

One was eight feet tall and still growing. She pointed to the loft. "Soon I will be able to see it from up there."

With scissors she cut a leaf off a smaller plant. When she handed it to me, it may have been the tail of a lizard. She said, "See the juice where I made the cut? Rub it on an open sore and you won't get an infection. It's a healing agent."

She put the ten-inch leaf into a plastic baggie, and handed it to me. She told me to put it in the refrigerator when I got home.

Each plant came from a different place. Hawaii, Georgia, France. Each plant had a story. She said, "It takes me two hours every morning to take care of them. As with children, each one must be treated according to its individual needs."

A moment passed, and she said, "Children shouldn't be raised as if on an assembly line. It's the same here."

I asked about the photographs on the wall. She pointed to a family photo. She was a young mother, pretty, her husband a big man who was bald at a young age. The children, a boy and girl, were school-age. She said, "We were married in Germany, after the war."

Next, she pointed to a picture of her son's Bar mitzvah. The next picture captured her daughter, who was striking. When she mentioned a divorce, I perked up. Her grand-children brought even more stories. The young girl's face inside the frame may have been flawless.

At her sister's photo, she only said, "She died."

Later, I saw the numbers on her arm.

*

One day, I saw her walking with groceries, each arm weighed down with a plastic bag. I chose not to take them from her, and let her struggle.

Each one of us defines our own dignity.

I said, "How are the plants?" Her eyes lit up with talk.

She said, "My daughter loves plants too, but she kills them. She lives around too many trees and there is no sunlight. My son also loves plants, but he doesn't understand them, the same way he fails with women."

Later in the conversation, she said, "In New York, my neighborhood got bad. My son wanted me to move by him."

She made a face.

"Bah! What is *Connecticut*? So I moved down here by my daughter. She drives me to the doctor, takes me to the mall. My son is a man. He tries, but doesn't know what to do."

*

Boud
avenue

In my father's house I can smell the wood, old now and rotting. I can smell the old memories suddenly kicking to the surface. It's the rug gurgling up ghosts. It's the smell of dog and old flannel.

Like the bird, I take my life with me wherever I go. Like the elephant, I am grounded, but in danger.

Already, I know how I will die.

*

Outside and next door, the neighbor rakes leaves into small piles. He talks to himself. Later, he will drag a plastic garbage bag from pile to pile, filling the bag. I heard him say, "That filthy Arab was in my shower again. I told them. I told them."

Continuing, he said, "I am not a hero. I'm just a man. I'm just a man. Forget that hero crap and give me back my son, General."

I called his last name, preceded by the word "mister".

He looked up.

I said, "Who am I?"

"Bobby Fischer."

There were no leaves. Later, we played "chess".

*

Inside, my father was resting in a chair. His dog lay on the floor under his meaty hand. Thick worker's fingers gently scratched the animal's belly. The dog's paws were in the air, and her eyes rolled back.

I would like to get my belly scratched. I would like to have no worries.

My sister comes in, to check his blood. There is a little machine. She pricks his finger, and he squeezes out a drop. The machine does the rest.

Then, she records the numbers in a notebook.
This happens three times a day.

⋆

I feel foolish around them. I am in the way. She is his care-taker now. I am only his son. I said, "The Mets are gaining steam."

"I don't watch that crap any more."

⋆

I let the dogs out, and go outside with them. They take off running. Over the fence, I see the little girl who had a crush on me. She is twenty-five now.

I walk over.

She said, "I didn't know you go to the meetings."

I said, "I was there to support a friend."

"You were alone."

"He was outside."

⋆

She showed me her finger, and the ring weighing it down.

I said, "You can't hold your hand up."

She beamed, "I know!"

I said, "Is he good to you?"

She said, "He has a job."

⋆

She was blonde, and tossed her hair. "Remember when I tried to kiss you? And you pushed me down?"

"You fell."

She said, "All the guys held you down, and I planted one right there. Remember? We were kids."

I said, "I was thirteen. You were six. You can understand."

"Do you want to kiss me now?"

"Yes," I said.

"But you can't," she said.

"Now," she said. "I get to push you down."

*

With both hands, she rubbed a non-existent belly. She said, "Someday I'll be fat. Will you want to kiss me then?"

"Fat?" I said. "Or pregnant?"

A man walked out. He was tall and thick. When he smiled, her knees buckled.

*

That evening at the dinner table, one of my nephews stumbled in drunk. My sister left the table immediately and their voices were loud from the other room.

My brother-in-law shook his head. He stabbed a piece of meat with his fork, and said, "She's too easy on them."

My father grunted, but kept eating.

I said, "He's sixteen. He's supposed to come home drunk once in a while."

My brother-in-law looked up sharply. "Third time this week. Also, he's not doing well in school. His grades are down and he gets in fights."

*

When my sister returned, nothing was said. Soon, we could hear the water running in the bathroom. Minutes after that, the front door slammed.

My sister sipped her drink. She said, "It's a phase."

*

After dinner, I took a walk. My feet were the slowest motors, and together we traced lines on a map. By now, old haunts failed to stir me. They were just old haunts, just old places where my tiny dramas once played out, where my old co-stars were nowhere to be found.

It was somebody else's turn. Somebody else's world now. Youth is a sad dream gone by the morning.

By the railroad tracks, I saw my nephew. He was with friends. They were smoking, and he offered it. I took one drag and passed it back.

It was strong.

The train whistle blew and one of them took off running. The kid yelled, "My stash! I left it on one of the rails!"

A little while later, we were walking down Main Street. His friends were gone. His feet scuffed along the sidewalk, the hem of his jeans frayed to white and well past his sneakers. A pickup roared past, its engine loud and raw because the muffler was missing. The driver honked the horn wildly and called my nephew's name.

My nephew responded with a nod.

He passed the cigaret.

Each of his movements was slower than the last. We were winding down.

We kept walking. The town was quiet, and the post office was closing. Maria from the drugstore crossed the street. She walked like she knew men were watching. My nephew said, "That one. In a couple of years I'll be ready for her."

*

Happy

I used to work with her. She asked when I was coming back and I told her never. She said, "Everyone is worried."

I said, "Everyone?"

She said, "Me."

*

In her apartment, she made dinner. Her daughter was at her sister's. Afterward, on the couch, I said, "It's nice like this. I get so tired, you know, of everything. But I'm not allowed to let it show."

I had stretched my arms out across the back of the couch. She sat in the rocking chair. Her lips moved. "Who told you that?"

"I was taught to be somebody else."

Later, she stroked my brow. Her body was warm against mine, and she was soft. I felt a calm come over me. With her hand on my chest, she said, "You must know I've thought about having your baby."

I said, "I have not always been a good son."

*

It was a nice apartment. The neighbors were quiet, and there was a lovely patio with a rose garden. She said, "No one ever comes down here and I don't know why."

I said, "What should we do with our time?"

We brought out wine, and carried candles. Softly I played the acoustic guitar, while, softly, she sang.

Later, upstairs on the small balcony, it began to snow, just a little at first. Large flakes drifted down without a pattern. They were all different, but all the same when they landed. It is this way with people, too, the different lives we live, only to end all the same, when we land.

She said, "My mother never loved me. She used to tell me. As far back as I can remember, she said I would never be happy. She said I was just like my father."

I asked, "Are you happy now?"

She said, "Yes."

"Then you win."

*

I told her, "I once found a friend in the yellow pages after years without any contact. When I asked him what happened, he shrugged."

She unbuttoned the top buttons of my shirt, and slid her hand inside. Finding enough hair to wrap her finger around, she pulled. I winced. She grinned.

I said, "He just got tired of me."

My friend from the phone book had told me one day that he was moving out of state. I never heard from him again. Then, a year later, while I was looking for a phone number, I came across his name.

I dialed the number. When he picked up, I said, Mitch?

Yes, he said.

I thought you moved.

Nope.

Do you want to get a beer?

Not really, he said, and hung up.

I told her, "Sooner or later you will get tired of me. Maybe that's what your mother meant. No one is ever happy *for very long*."

*

Her father was a drummer in different blues bands. He traveled a lot when she was young, and didn't always send money home. Her mother began to hate him. When she started to see more of her daughter in him than in herself, she began to hate her too.

I asked, "Is she still alive?"

"Yes."

"Should we visit?"

"Well, she has guns and only one good eye now."

*

I was in bed. There was a commotion at the front door. Staggering out in sweatpants, I saw a man. He held her by the wrist. We looked at each other.

He let her go.

Later, after a shower, I asked, "Who was that?"

Quietly, she said, "The last one."

*

She liked to cook for me. One night, she attempted a new recipe, one which demanded some extra skill. She invited friends of hers, a couple.

Stan was an actor who made low-budget films. Liz worked for a clothier. At the table, Stan suggested a game where the women would compete against the men. At first I was enthusiastic. Soon, it became a variation of Truth Or Dare.

The Truth had to do with the two women, embraced and their lips touching.

The Dare had to do with Stan and me.

I took my clothes off first. When Stan removed his, it became obvious the nature of the films he had made.

*

That night, I dreamed a wild woman bit off my penis. She held it in her mouth proudly, her head high, as if a bird-dog displaying a fine retrieval. Her tail even wagged.

In the morning, the sheets were bloody. And I was reminded.

*

She liked the way I rubbed her clitoris with the flat end of my tongue, and would hold my head there. I tried to make her moan louder each time. She bit her lip, and said, "The neighbors!"

In the days that followed, I would see people in the hallway. The women would sneer, while the men would grin.

I enjoyed the celebrity of being with a woman who screams when my penis is inside her.

*

At a club, an older man sweated behind a drum kit. He was balding but his hair was cut short. He was muscular and a vein in his scalp bulged. His chin hair reminded me of the cool cats from the Fifties, the ones whose books I still read when I am feeling staid and incomplete.

It reminds me I am not *supposed* to be *anybody*. I only need to live as I go, and end up where I end up. It reminds me that I will *always* be incomplete. It is the nature of being human.

After the set, he sat at our table. They joined hands, and she smiled. Looking at me, he said to her, "This is him?"

I told him, "I believe the blues will one day cure cancer."

He said, "Do you drink?"

"My father was a Dewar's man."

*

Daddy called a woman to our table. She was older, and her breasts threatened to leave the blouse in shreds. She wrung her hands, and tried to look innocent. Soon, they were both on stage, the woman singing soulfully from a place deep inside.

I watched her throat, how it bulged with words, and then became narrow when it was empty. When I went to the men's room, Daddy appeared next to me. With both of us hanging out, he said, "She's my daughter, but she's crazy. Don't say I didn't warn you."

He zipped up, and left without washing.

In the morning, a drive into town was decided. After a few miles, she stopped the car. "Get out. You can't live with me any more."

I held out my hands.

When she was gone, I told myself, "Your mother was right, and so was your father."

*

Kill

The first thing he said over the phone was, "What is she wearing?" I told him to stop calling me at work. He uses me as his spy. Gently, I say, "It's been three months."

Just as gently, he says, "I'm dying."

*

When he called again, his voice was slightly deeper, and raspy. I said, "Have you been sleeping?"

He said, "I've been following her. Yesterday, she got into a strange car. They drove to a restaurant. I watched them through the window. She had the chicken."

*

A few days later I was in his apartment. He'd been drinking. There was a smell, which at first I could not place. It was familiar, like an uncle in a hat pulled down over his eyes. At first you think he is your father.

Then I realized that in another room, something had been burned.

A little while later he sifted through a pile of ashes. Hoarsely, he said, "Pictures."

*

In the chair, his knees were crossed. He pointed to several white stretched patches of skin. Over time, the skin had hardened. "Dog bites," he said, "from when I was a kid. So you can see why today I am afraid of dogs."

He covered his chest with a hand, and said, "My heart. So you can see why women terrify me."

I said, disgusted, "You are acting like one."

He poured drinks from a bottle on the table, and read a poem. Later, I would vomit.

He said, "Do you think they're having sex?"

He answered his own question, with the face of someone who had just received a fist to the gut. He walked across the room and pulled open a drawer. Inside, there was a long Japanese knife, the kind used for hari-kari. He said, "I am considering my options."

He called the cat over. With a flick of the wrists, the tip of the cat's tail was gone. I gathered my coat, and pulled my arms through the sleeves. Droplets of blood showed me the way to the door.

He held the knife out in front of him so the blade end was ready to enter his belly-button. As I was closing the door, I saw the cat again. It was missing an ear.

⋆

When I was a kid, maybe ten, one of my neighbor friends caught a frog. Breathless, he came up to me with his hands cupped, one over the other. His eyes were firecrackers. When he opened his hands, the frog was dead.

He had run all the way home from school with it.

Years later, I tell my friend, "Be careful what you love."

⋆

When I was in kindergarten, my sister was in eighth grade. My mother insisted she walk me to school. So every morning we stopped at my sister's friend's house, next to the railroad tracks, and the three of us walked together.

The boys would tease us, and say we were stupid.

One morning, my sister had found a small blue egg. It had fallen out of a tree. Soon it was decided this was a robin's egg. She wrapped it in a tissue and gave it to me. When the boys teased, my sister said, "If we're so stupid, how come we got a robin's egg and all you got is a dirty face!"

She said to me, "Show them."

I took out the egg.

After school, I put the egg in my sock drawer and waited for it to hatch. One morning weeks later my mother said, "What smells in here?"

My egg was soon discovered.

When my mother asked me what I was doing with a rotting blue egg, I told her everything I knew. I said, "It's better than having a dirty face."

*

In school, during gym, the game "Kill" was invented. We were supposed to play soccer but there was a rag on the field. It had been part of a white tee-shirt.

One of the boys picked it up, and immediately like a pack of wolves the other boys "attacked". It was ten on one each time. Whoever pulled the rag from the pile was "it".

Instinctively, the rules made themselves.

It was simple.

If you possessed the rag, you had to run for your life. But you had to have the rag in order to win. Later, in class and out of breath, bruised and bleeding, we argued over who had it the longest.

The girls stood off to the side, bored, watching. Such is the pool of future husbands and fathers at seven years old.

Such is the pool now, years later. Women still watch men, trying to choose the least rotten egg.

*

When I was young, my mother had ideas.

At the dinner table, she would go around asking each of us about our day. At that point we were required to give a full account. She would eye us, ready to lacerate any lie or half-truth with her wit, which was subtle as a butterfly but also deadly as a howitzer.

Once, I told her, "I met the girl I will marry. But she made me mad, so I made her scream."

I was eleven.

Somewhere inside the birth sac I had acquired the same wit, except for one very distinct difference. My mother liked balloons. I liked popping them.

*

If my mother were alive I would show her my hands, and say, "See? No pins."

A man from China told me about regrets. He said they are too flimsy to hold up to the sun, and too heavy to carry around. It's best to leave them in the road and keep walking.

⋆

My jealous friend pounded on my front door. Crawling out of bed, I answered in my underwear. He barged in.

Sweating, he said, "I need bus fare to Boston! She's marrying him!"

I told him to sit down. Nervous, he rubbed his bouncing knee, while startled, I rummaged through my wallet. He was bleeding.

⋆

Issues

I walked into town, where there was a commotion. Two college kids had stopped traffic. They had an American flag, and matches. Soon, the flag was in flames.

Some men leaped from a pickup truck. There were fists, and people yelling. Faces were contorted, and it seemed like their words appeared in bubbles over their heads like in the comics. I tried, but couldn't make out the captions.

I get bored easily, and walked past it.

When I dug my hands in my pockets I found some coins. I placed them in the road, between the double yellow lines.

A woman saw me. She was in her 50s. "Why did you do that?" she said.

I told her, "Nothing's free."

*

In a restaurant I sat at the counter and ordered coffee. The waitress asked me where I lived. "I don't live," I tell her.

The cake she brought was stale.

Two men talked in a booth, a man with a hat and a man with a scarf. The Hat said, "My son got caught in the wrong place at the wrong time."

The Scarf said, "My daughter is sorry about the baby. In the dictionary it says an execution is putting someone to death. In other words, a decision."

The Hat said, "I no longer feel like voting."

The Scarf picked at his plate, and said, "These eggs are cold."

A kid came in from the street. His jacket was pulled out and his hair was messy. He was bleeding from the nose. Somebody asked. Pulling a napkin from the holder, and patting his nose, he said, "It's the president again. He keeps punching me in the face."

Another kid came in, with a baseball bat. Breathing fire.

*

Woman
in mink coat

Sundays are my battle. I get depressed and drink. I get sad for no explainable reason. I become anxious, and lose myself in self-doubt and the idea that one day I will die.

It has been this way since I was young.

Over the years, I have attempted to attribute this Sunday queasiness to one thing or another. Finally, I decided this proves reincarnation. I figured I must have had a terrible tragedy occur in a previous life – on a Sunday.

But who was I, and what happened?

Did I meet an ugly end on a Sunday? Was I butchered like a cow by a mass murderer in the Thirties? Was I hitch-hiking across Kansas, looking for work, with only my horn to my name, and stepped into the wrong car?

Did it go further back, and I was shot on a foreign battlefield, and lay there for days before dying?

Or even further, and I was beheaded in a king's court for being a scamp, or languished in a dungeon with no hope of seeing the sun? Then I remembered what happened to me on a Sunday. I was *born* on a Sunday.

Plagued by the musings of troubled men, I decided to go for a walk.

*

In town, the cars went in slow-motion. It was cold. I wore a thin jacket, and shivered. A woman walked down the street in a mink coat. She stopped, sneered, and said, "I don't like how you look at me."

I had been thinking about buying a car, so I crossed the street, where there was a used-car lot. The man there had crooked teeth, and since mine were crooked also, I trusted him immediately.

After we chatted a while about the new experimental cars, he rolled his tongue and said, "My father had another thing coming if he thought

I was going to college."

I told him, "I didn't go to college, either."

He said, "So I sell cars."

I said, "I sell myself short."

⋆

"So, what do you know about women?" I asked.

"I know enough to keep my mouth shut when they're around. Now, follow me."

In the back room, he ran a film projector. "Don't look closely," he smirked. "You might see your grandmother."

I said, "These are from the forties, right?"

"Yes."

"All these people are dead."

⋆

He pulled out a drawer, and slammed the bottle on the desk. Pouring out two drinks perfectly, he muttered, "My father had the right idea."

I knocked mine back.

"Look," he said. "The bottom line is we will always be their sons."

⋆

In a diner, I took a booth seat by a window and watched traffic. I told the waitress coffee. I told her my name. I tried to smile.

The blur of cars and trucks outside caused a minor glitch in my own navigational system. In the fumes I thought I saw my parents holding hands.

My old poet friend who lives two towns over was sitting at the counter. He was eating pie, and chatting up the waitress. Half his age, she was staring off. Her eyes were glazed over.

I was noticed, and he waved a hand.

In my booth now, we sat with coffee. He shook his head, and said, "I cut my hair. I'm not Jesus any more."

"Mine's falling out," I told him, dividing my part with my hands. "Look."

Once, I had worshipped him. In my twenties he had me convinced we were starting a revolution. His soapbox was heavily constructed and reinforced in all the inappropriate places. He liked to shake his fist, and spit when he talked. What he was looking for was an audience.

Often in those days, up in his little garage apartment, I clapped vigorously.

*

Back then, in a state of imaginary intellectualism, I had said, "Fiction is dead. The paragraph is a dinosaur. The sentence is an old maid. All the words have been around forever. Somebody needs to spit in the milk."

There were drawings on the thin walls, and photographs of his young wife in black lingerie and pout. There were books stacked in corners, high as the ceiling. They teetered like towers on bad footing. They wobbled like drunks.

A large banner of a sunflower hung out the window. Blake's dream of life, his life of dream.

I lounged on his couch a lot then, while he'd hunker down in his beat-up old chair, a cup of coffee in both hands. From these hallowed vantage points, we mused over politics and religion. We lamented the dizzyingly repressed sexual relations between man and woman in modern society.

He was writing a book called, "Outside The Fascist Church." While I was writing one called, "American Suicide."

We rode bikes to the ocean and played tennis until we passed out. We talked about how to save literature and how poetry would save the world.

A revolution was in front of us, and we were its two main components.

*

One night, a man and his wife, both in their 60s, came over for coffee. The man was a musician, woodwinds mostly, and had known one of the Beats. He played music while my poet friend and I read poems we had written.

There was a tape recorder.

My first one was good, about Kerouac in a bar, how his arms weren't long enough to reach the one thing in life he truly needed. I could hear the flute behind me sing. I could feel my heart soar. The second one bombed, and there was silence. Quietly, the musician laid his flute down. His wife looked at me oddly.

Awkward, my friend said, "I'm not sure how to follow that."

Things soon collapsed.

That night I realized, "I am not who I think I am."

The aftermath of any event is often an empty shell. It's only natural. My friend put one of his mother's Enrico Caruso records on his son's Fisher-Price record-player. One of the pictures had fallen. There was glass. He went for a broom.

He had wanted to be Jesus, but the bread in my stomach sat there like a stone.

At one point, when I told him I was happy finally, he disapproved. He said, "I like you when you're sad. You're a better writer when you're miserable."

*

Now, in the diner booth, he asked me about my life. Before I could answer, he was telling me about *his* life. Bored, I said, "I think I just heard the sound of one hand clapping."

I left money on the counter, and was walking out.

He called, "You know, you never materialized."

Stopping in the doorway, I filled my pockets. I waited. I rolled my eyes.

He went on, and said, "At one point you were the franchise. I was grooming you. Now, look at you."

Either that's what he said, or that's what I heard. I have always been hard on myself.

I left.

In the street, the lady in the mink coat was still walking. She was in traffic now, angry and confused. She stepped into a pickup, and the tires squealed. I stared at the sun until it blinded me. In the spots, I saw her clearly.

*

In my
building

The girl in the apartment next door was funny that way. She was never in town, and when she was, when I saw her car parked in her assigned space in the lot, the shower would run for hours. I mean, *hours*.

I would listen for the water running. At that point, I knew she was naked on the other side, with only a tiled wall between us. Immediately, I would tear off my clothes and hop into my own shower. Somehow, this made us closer.

I would touch myself, pretending my hands were hers. When I closed my eyes, I imagined other things. I would tongue-kiss the wall. I would press myself, my hardness against the coolness. Still, I felt the heat.

In the hallway I would mention her array of sweaters. Once, I saw her digging in the dumpster, and quipped. "You know, people will talk."

She smiled thinly and told me she threw out some bills.

"Don't worry, they'll send more."

Pushing up my sleeves, I offered help, and then plunged an arm into the refuse. After several false alarms, I found the lost bounty, and pulled out the plastic bag. She was mildly grateful, and held the door for me.

In the hallway again, she said, "Men frighten me. My father was a goat."

I said, "I have no interest in reading you bedtime stories."

She mentioned music, and I said Miles Davis. She said, "That hack." Seconds later, it was over between us.

*

My friend came by. He said, "I hate who I am."

I told him, "America was once ruled by religious freaks."

He said, "Once?"

We peeled peanuts on the patio as the sun was going down. He said, "No one knows the truth. I mean, how could she believe it? Sometimes she has the mind of a child, but I guess that's what I like about her too."

There was a squirrel. I tossed a peanut and he took it in his paws. He looked side to side, and darted up a vine.

*

I had put a record on my borrowed turn-table. It scratched and hissed, and there were secret messages hidden in every skip. When we played it backwards, the cryptic voice instructed us to eat baloney.

*

In order to get girls, I once pretended to be shiftless. It ended badly. One of them was sad for me, and said, "This isn't you."
My friend said, "I love white women. People get mad."

*

He was a musician, and had a different girl in every city. It got to where he stopped calling them by their first names, and only knew them by the city they lived in. For instance, St. Louis was a leggy blonde who liked to sew.
Cleveland was loyal to the locals, and in the morning made French Toast in the nude.
N'Awlins was a wild woman who killed chickens raw.
Hackensack liked yard sales and had sore feet.
Oakland was faux city.
New Mexico was earthy, and had a way of rolling her R's that loosened the male spine.
All the girls from San Francisco were poets, or wished they were, or wanted to lie down with them.
All the girls from Milwaukee drooled when they talked about Elvis and Harley Davidsons.
I wasn't good enough to play with the band, and only played to the audience of my own four walls. I stood up there like I owned the place, and blew my trumpet with all my might.
Ultimately, I had skills.
Judging from the reaction of my neighbors, I knew how to boil blood.

*

My friend played jazz guitar, beautifully so his fingers never seemed to move. At times I thought I was dreaming.

When the neighbors yelled up, I stamped my feet and yelled down, "I bet you thought Charlie Christian was dead."

*

My friend took off his shoes, and then his socks. He wriggled his toes. The big one was deformed, and I asked.

He said, "An accident when I was a kid. I don't like talking about it."

I told him, "My goal is to one day be a recluse. Until then, people talk to each other."

He got mad, and then I did too.

At one point, his guitar got sticky with alcohol. I apologized, and he threw it back at me. He said, "You don't do anything. All you do is talk."

He put his socks on.

*

I had wanted to tell him, "I don't just talk. Later, I write it down and call it a book."

But I said nothing.

I put the tv on. Gilligan was pissing off The Skipper again.

*

At four-thirty in the morning, the fire alarm on my floor went off. I could hear doors opening and closing. Accordingly, the ringing would dampen and rise. At first, I thought it was someone's alarm clock, coupled with indecision at the front door.

The welcome mat was burning.

The fire extinguisher could not distinguish between a hat and a coat.

The ringing went on for thirty minutes, and I became annoyed.

Finally, I pulled my head from under the pillow and grabbed my glasses. Pulled on sweatpants, and opened the door. There were two cops, one of them female, and the super all roaming the floor. The cops had flashlights and were knocking on doors. "Is your smoke alarm going off? Is there smoke in your apartment?"

On one door the super pounded a fist. Groggy, he said, "Pam? Are you alright in there?"

Pam was older, and heavy, and had trouble getting around. Often, I would see her in the stairwell struggling with grocery bags, and I would help. The male officer told her it was the police. He asked if she smelled smoke.

Startled, she said, "The police? I'm not dressed!"

The male cop said, "We have a woman here."

Finally, I went back to sleep. My friend was gone, but had left his shoes. Later, Crazy Paul from the second floor asked if he could have them.

*

My next door neighbor came by, freshly showered. She wore a sweater which made my heart beat faster. Her hair fell long down her back. As she passed, she told me to "have a good one."

I wanted to teach her life.

I wanted to tell her everything I knew.

It wouldn't take long.

Instead, I watched her disappear down the stairs. My tongue felt fat in my mouth. It clogged the words, and killed my babies.

*

On the beach, with my hood up, the sky began to lighten. The seagulls waited for the sun. We waited together. I needed to let my sullenness become my personality. I needed to find a new way of unraveling. This time the pieces wouldn't matter. Every epiphany has a starting point.

An old man came jogging up. He was 80 and I often saw him in the mornings. He kept a prayer list in his pocket, and had added my father's name to it months ago.

Mostly, we knew each other by nods.

He ran past.

The seagulls were brazen. One walked up next to me. The wind blew back his feathers, like it blew back my hair. Together, we watched the sun come up. Later, he would scrounge for food, while I would scrounge for time.

I picked up shells, most of them broken, and tossed them in the tide for the edges to soften. In a hundred years, they would be jewels.

In a hundred years, I might be too.

The epiphany would have to come another day. Or possibly not at all. Or maybe just did. Despite the prayer list, my father was dead.

*

In the
poetry section

I met a girl in a bookstore, in the poetry section. We joked about how poor the selection was in the 'chain stores'. Soon, it was decided we should spend more time together, and coffee was suggested.

At the coffee shop, she told me about her little brother. He is deformed and slightly retarded. "My mother cries," she said.

I told her, "I was the youngest. Often, growing up, I felt deformed and slightly retarded. Perhaps it's his environment."

With no emotion, she said, "He walks around with urine running down his leg. One of his arms is six inches long."

⋆

In my apartment, we listened to records. She liked Motown the best, and we danced. At one point, she told me her age.

When I told her mine, she reached into her purse. Pulling out a rock, she said, "I found this weeks ago. I put it in my purse. I don't know why."

I said, "I know why."

I held out my hand.

I said, "Give me the rock. Tomorrow you will feel lighter."

She was skinny, and I wanted to feed her. I put water on for pasta, and brought out the wok for the shrimp. There was grease everywhere. I slipped, and we laughed. I poured two glasses of Grand Marnier, and we sat out on the balcony.

We could hear the ocean, and the moon was full and bright.

She said, "Mostly, men amuse me. But you're different."

I said, "How am I different?"

She said, "You want me to feel good about myself."

⋆

A
year of
jobs

A friend tipped me off. He said go down to the garbage company at four AM. He said bring an old pair of gloves and a bottle of water. It turned out they were always short-handed, and in no time I was on a truck.

I had to chase him down the parking lot, though, and hop in before he hit the highway.

The driver said, "You got all your teeth?"

I showed him.

He said, "Most of the boys come straight from County. It's all drunk-tank riff raff brought in from bar fights the night before. You know."

I said, "I don't know anything."

"How's your back?"

I told him, "I once held up my entire family for three years straight, without eating, sleeping, or leaving anything in the road behind me. I'm ready for anything."

He showed me how to stand on the back of the truck. How to operate the lever that crushed the garbage. He said, "Now, when we're driving, keep your head poked in. Some a these trees hang low and they'll get you. The road signs too, they come out a nowhere."

*

By ten AM, my back was ready to break. My hands reeked of fish and day-old pizza.

He took one look, squinted, and said, "You lied to me."

He asked if I wanted to drive for a while. When I didn't laugh at the joke, and then couldn't move, he knew I was useless the rest of the day.

He scratched his head.

He said, "I seen this before."

*

I was up on my feet, but my arms dragged along the ground. I felt as if I had just fallen out of a plane.

He said, "The office is a good ways from here. But there's a bus station not far up. You want, I could drop you there. You won't get paid, but you can go on home."

I declined his kind offer, pulled myself together, and climbed back on. We finished the day.

*

Back at the office, they owed me over-time. The boss said, "Come back tomorrow."

I said, "What's wrong with today?"

He pinched his cigaret, pulled it from his mouth. "Because I said tomorrow."

He knew I wouldn't be back tomorrow.

I left, but didn't have a ride, so started walking.

About a mile down the road, an old friend stopped. A woman I knew. She was pregnant, and her belly barely fit behind the steering wheel. She drove with a lead-foot.

She said, "You're not working for your father any more?"

I stared out the window.

She made a face. "You smell."

*

Monster
movie

I wore Halloween masks to work seven days in a row. On the eighth day I was asked why. I told them, "Because I am trying to show what a monster movie this is. I am interested in relaying my thoughts concerning the masks we all wear here every day, by making my masks very obvious."

My supervisor said, "I think you are a little high-minded for what we are trying to accomplish here."

I said, "This is a post office."

He said, "Exactly."

*

Later, I used the Ladies Room, unzipping without concern. One said, "Sir, that sink is for hands."

To which I said, "Well, here I have a foot."

To which, she replied, "Oh, hardly!"

*

Driving home one night, I had a passenger. I turned to her. "A drink? Also, I am famished."

She said, "*You're* driving."

In the morning, we were discreet.

*

There is no great brain power attached to matching the name and number on a slip of paper to the name and number on a box. My job diminishes a monkey. Some people, though, fit right in.

I see one now.

"Frank," I say. "Are you rolling around in your own feces again? You old hound dog. It smells like a barn in here."

I see another one.

"Mary," I call out. "When you were a little girl, you tortured small animals. Don't lie. It's in your eyes."

Still another one slumps through. I said, "Your Jesus complex is confusing. Are you the messiah or the misogynist?"

*

I wanted to see what would happen. I wanted to prove a theory. So one day I managed to take several clandestine pictures from a camera-phone. In secrecy, I discovered the truth.

Later, when I had the pictures transferred, I found a gallery of strangeness.

In one photo, the cat who lives in the parking lot was petting a bird. The cat was outstretched on the pavement. His paw was extended and curled, creating a cradle. Inside the cradle a small bird sat very still. The cat gently patted the bird on the head and back. The cat gently licked the bird, cleaning it as it would clean itself.

Soon, the bird flew off.

*

In another photo, a supervisor extended his arm around a female co-worker, cradling her. In what he wrongfully assumed was a private moment, he cupped one of her breasts. He patted her on the head, and licked her face.

Soon, she flew off.

*

Other photos depicted the janitor urinating into the microwave. The boss shoving pot-roast down his pants. His boss straightening his wig with chop-sticks.

I was finding nothing out of the ordinary, nothing I didn't already know.

Until the last photo.

*

There used to be a television in the break-room. On that television, I watched the second plane plunge into the second tower.

At some point the post master removed the cable for expense reasons.

By working this job, I realize I am missing out on history.

*

I met a woman at a party for a co-worker. She was recently graduated with a PhD. She was young, her dark hair was shiny, and she still had that baby-fresh smell. Sharing her expertise on my personal condition, the words slipped out of her mouth like worms.

According to her, I was a typical case.

In essence, my dissatisfaction with my job had more to do with my dissatisfaction with myself. In other words, I would be unhappy anywhere. She said, "To put it plainly, you hate to work. You should explore that."

I told her what she could explore.

*

The drink in my hand brought on another learned conclusion from our visiting medical dignitary. She said, "Do you often sublimate such feelings of rage with alcohol. Some men choose a series of females. Some men fight. But your method speaks to a stagnancy of spirit. I wonder, do you also have impotency problems?"

Her lips pressed together more tightly by the second. She seemed to lightly gag on each new sentence.

At the last line, she blinked very rapidly.

I became smug. I told her, "You're too skinny for me."

*

She went on. "Violence is a passion, taken in a certain direction. A violent man is often good in bed."

I mentioned my work fantasy.

"Go on," she said.

"I want to plunge a pair of scissors straight into the black heart of my supervisor."

She cuddled up next to me, purring. "So what are you doing later?"

*

After several dates I had the idea that we should spend the weekend together. Once the initial newness wore off, she stopped analyzing me and initiated a less cerebral approach to our closeness.

She nibbled warmly on the inside of my thighs, while I grasped for the meaning of all this by holding her hair. By the end of the weekend we had an understanding. I was a hopeless self-destructive. She, in turn, was intent on saving me.

Her main method of rescue was oral sex.

I went along with it.

Sunday night she made an announcement. "I think it would be prudent if we continued this experiment on a weekly basis. Our bodies are teachers."

I touched her hair, wrapped it around my fingers until I could feel her skull pull towards me. Taut in my grip, she knew who was boss. I pulled her face right up to mine. I said, "Is this what you mean?"

She was sweating.

*

Later, when I was at her mercy, she made a face. She said, "I only want good people in my life. So you can see why I'm not sure about this."

She had gained power over me because I "liked" her.

She left teeth-marks on the physical, but also psychological, manifestation of my being.

*

Several co-workers sat around a table. I had been at this bar numerous times before. The bartender knew me, and nodded. A joke was made at his expense, which I didn't appreciate.

A woman I had hard feelings for was sitting across from me. As part of the general conversation, she said, "I think it's better to steal than to lie."

Often, I don't know what to say in situations. So, I said nothing. So, I sipped my drink. But soon, very quietly, I told her, "In the past, you have stolen from me and then lied about it. Where do you stand on that?"

She said she was a baseball player, covering all her bases. She eyed me. "How many kids do *you* have at home?"

*

Later she bought me a drink, which I accepted. Her girlfriend then began talking about their encounters. The girlfriend sat in the middle chair at the table, and her blouse was low-cut.

Her eyes screamed out, *Look at me! Everyone must look at me!*

She beamed.

The married women at the table disapproved. The single men listened with rapt attention. This of course is nature.

★

The girlfriend resembled one of Ernest Hemingway's granddaughters.

I remembered most of his best books. I have never thought much of bullfights, but shotguns intrigue me when aimed just right, and long stretches of drinking wine in European bars and bistros strikes an especially illustrious chord. The whole fish scenario though seemed a bit drab in the larger scheme of things.

Follow the blood, is what I learned from that one. This will lead you to the source.

She said, "I can't keep up with her. She's a machine. Well, not a machine. A machine has an off switch. I most love what she does with her mouth. I am glistening as we speak."

★

A little while later, while I was immersed in a separate conversation, my hands were mentioned. "They're so big around that little glass," she said. "It makes me wonder if you're a monster or not."

"I find it impossible to believe," I told her, "that no man would want you."

I followed her plunging neckline. She said, "You can stop looking. Those aren't for you."

"I was hoping to find another reason for this," I told her. "I was looking for why people treat each other badly, when life is so short. I was looking for these things somewhere down between the cleavage of a woman who would never have anything to do with me."

We exchanged grins.

One of the women came back from the bathroom, the brand new drugs just beginning to sort out her nervous system.

It was mentioned. There was a dirty look.

⋆

In the parking lot, I followed one of the women to her car. She had whispered in my ear as she was leaving, "Walk me out."

The pavement seemed very flexible under my feet. I was contemplating a new direction in life, but had only vague ideas and premonitions at that point. Plus, I was convinced there was more there than meets the eye.

She pointed to a small dog trotting across the parking lot. In the moonlight we could see its ribs. She motioned toward it, and took a step.

It ran off.

The last photo had something to do with this, only the dog was a man. The last photo was me.

⋆

~

'We used His nails
to build our house...'

Crazy
art

Consider this.

Not every suicide is true. In order to find out if you can fly, sometimes you have to jump off a building.

*

I think my personality makes it necessary that I live alone. As for any potential life-mate, I either scare her off, or make her uneasy. If she stays around too long then *I* get uneasy.

The vicious circle laps itself many times over. The flames bite at my ankles.

It's not on purpose, my aloof nature, although it may be subconscious. My New Year resolution is to look people in the eye. Theirs should be to look back.

*

I wanted to play my trumpet in a way that people would notice, and say, "Yes, this is familiar to me. I understand this."

I wanted to put into sound what I have already put into words. I wanted to make an expression beyond my control. I wanted to make a beautiful noise.

In the park, I held the instrument like a gunslinger, down against my leg. I was standing slightly slanted. I was squinting in the sun. I was waiting for someone to say, "Draw!"

A woman walked her dog. She said, "Is that thing just for show?"

I smacked my lips against the mouthpiece, and pretended to spit out a bit of paper stuck on the tip of my tongue. The dog dropped his ears, as if being punished.

The woman winced.

I am now a man of the vine. Once, I drank whiskey like water. Once, I inhaled vodka and that beautifully spiced rum. But there is a culprit lurking around now. There is a villain in my life.

Today, I am a wino.

High blood pressure, you cur!

*

My friend says, "Why don't you just stop drinking altogether?" The new burst of smoke she blows out meets the last burst, which has not yet dissipated. They form to create an atomic bomb cloud in my apartment.

I said, "I have to share myself with the universe now. A radio was playing in a dream I had. At one point I realized it was reacting to me. It was playing what it thought I wanted to hear, instead of what it wanted to play. I have to be conscientious now more than ever of all things around me, because I am a part of all things around me, and so therefore I affect all things around me. This is not my ego talking, this is how it is for all of us. I see it now."

The chimney eyed me. Her eyes were wet and red from the smoke. Her cigaret hand rocked.

*

Another friend, concerned with my weight, says, "It's about self control." He then tells me about the last three girls he's cheated with.

Surrounded by weakness, I give up.

All I can offer back is more weakness.

*

A third friend discusses the merits of "discipline". At first, I'm not sure what she means. Finally, she says, "For instance, I could crack you into shape."

With her thin left hand, she made a whipping motion.

Ooh, a southpaw.

*

On my Sunday walk into town, I took a different route than usual. In the street, by the curb, there were several nails. I picked up the nails and tossed them into the grass. Then, considering lawnmowers, I removed the potential projectiles.

I would up putting the nails in my pocket.

*

A little later, as I passed the bank, a pickup truck pulled to the curb. The door opened, and a woman I at first mistook for a man stepped out. Soon, a little boy with a Mohawk haircut was running around. Dying next to the lamppost was a Christmas tree someone had thrown away.

A single strand of tinsel remained.

The woman said, "Go ahead. Take it."

When the boy hesitated, *she* grabbed it. "Snooze you lose, kid."

She tossed the tree in the back of the truck. The tires screeched. A man coming out of the bank dropped his wallet. As he picked it up, he gave me a dirty look. He said, "Who do you think you are?"

*

In the book store, the aisles were narrow. The store was divided into two rooms, connected by a doorway. In one half the shelves were filled with fancy bars of homemade soap, scented oils, and many small *knick-knacks* with the name of the town on it.

A woman said to a man, "What I would do to you with these oils!"

The man rolled his eyes, and she pressed against him. "Show me," he whispered back. Quietly, they purchased the oils.

The other half of the store was all books. It was Sunday and crowded. People were quiet, and no one said hello. I picked up an Amy Hempel book and read the first page. When my path out was blocked by another reader, I went around the other way because I hate to be a bother.

*

If I was dying from a disease, I would keep it to myself. I wouldn't want a big send off. No farewell tour for me. I have always lived my life in the background. I have always conversed with the shadows.

I hate to be a bother.

I am a hypochondriac too, and always think I am dying. This much is true, though. One day, I will be right.

I felt the need to be part of something. On the way home from a place in my mind, I carried nails in my pocket. I saw three men in the distance. Distressed, one of them waved to me.

When I ran up, I could see they were holding up a roof. Their arms were giving out, and beginning to buckle. I quickly applied my nails. Later, my back was sore because of all the pats.

My cheeks hurt because of smiling back at them.

I was invited inside. Beer bottles clinked, and one smashed. A woman rushed over with a towel. I watched her bend. Her hair was long, and the tips got wet.

In the other room, I dried them for her. My hand roamed down her spine. I played the knots like a trumpet and she made a beautiful noise.

There was a wall fixture of Jesus on the Cross, only the Jesus was missing. I said, "What happened?"

She rubbed my chest with the flat of her palm. "Don't you remember, silly? We used His nails to build our house."

*

When we were alone, she cooked dinner while I sifted through her record collection. My mood took effect at the same time the record did.

We moved slowly to the music.

At some point the walls danced, and the dog talked, all the clichés became alive. They rummaged through our closets. They made us tell the truth. She said, "My mother never loved me. But she was a stellar performer, and did it in ways that no one else could see. I was raised by a psychopath. You see now why I am alone."

I told her, "My mother died for my sins."

We took off all our clothes and sat intertwined in the bathtub. She said, "The lady who lived here before me killed herself in this tub. Every Sunday, it backs up. It turns out ghosts are a quirky bunch."

Rubbing my fingers against her body, I said, "You are soft. Not rubbery at all."

She said, "I was in a convent for a year. It had to do with my father wanting me for himself. I grew up strange."

At one point, I said, "Are we doing drugs? I can't tell any more."

*

Later, I recited Allen Ginsberg poetry, or made it up. She played my horn. The dog was gone. On the stove, the food had burnt and smoke poured out like an overheated car engine.

The smoke alarm rang for the next thirteen hours before we figured out how to turn it off. After a while it became a song. Our song. Our wedding song without the wedding. She said, "You smell like barbed wire."

"What does that mean?"

"I don't know. But I think I should be careful with you. What do you think?"

*

I think I am always jumping off buildings. Maybe I can fly. Maybe you will catch me. Maybe we will make crazy art on the sidewalk, when we hit. Maybe it takes a crazy girl to see me for who I am.

*

House
for sale

At a red light, she jumped in my car. She pointed in a direction and I let my foot off the brake. "Turn here," she said.

In an abandoned building, there was a baby. The baby wasn't breathing. "I wanted to show you this," she said.

*

In a hospital, in the maternity ward, a room of babies cried. They were tired and cranky from the trip. Dressed in pink and blue, they wriggled uncomfortably. They wore wristbands. Without the wristbands they would not exist.

Their names were on the wristbands.

Their families.

Their owners.

If the wristbands were lost, or somehow switched, an entire existence would be altered. Such is the helpless nature of newborns. They are at our mercy.

Later, in old age, there will be hell to pay.

*

I had dinner with friends. We drank and laughed and talked about work. The waitress had a tiny smile, which was noticed. My female friend said, "I bet the men never leave her alone."

Then she said, "What is she, twelve?"

A couple walked in with a baby. The baby was sleeping. Small bubbles had formed on his lips, and his smile was tiny. My female friend grew silent.

Her husband squeezed her hand.

*

Later, the beach held us up, as our feet sunk into the sand. The moon was nearly full and looked like a man in a hat just as a lady was passing.

A fire was built.

A bottle appeared.

*

My female friend was lying in the sand. Her legs were spread. She dug a hole until her arm was in elbow-deep. Each time she would bring out her cupped hand, it was filled with cool dark sand.

"What's down there?" I asked.

"I don't know yet. I'm not deep enough," she said.

*

The next day, at another light, the same woman jumped into my car. We drove and turned and walked up stairs. In the abandoned house, in a room, was a small boy. His face was dirty.

He pointed to the floor.

On an oval throw-rug, a dog was sleeping. But it wasn't a dog. It was a picture of a dog. The boy was eating the crayons he had used to draw it. He couldn't talk because he didn't know any words.

The picture growled at me. The boy foamed at the mouth.

*

The next time I was in that house, the boy was older. His arm was bruised. His hair was long or it was dirty or it was both.

The window was rotted, and glass had shattered. A bird was dead.

Sometimes a bird will fly right into a window because he doesn't know it's there. This may explain why I bump into people in the street.

They usually say a dirty word, the people, which I collect into jars. Always, I poke holes in the lid so the words breathe. Once, they escaped and the whole neighborhood was infuriated with each other.

*

Music came from another room. When I opened the door, I saw only vinyl record albums. The albums were spread on the floor, a few of them spilling out of their covers.

In a rocking chair, my mother wept.

I said to no one, "Whose house is this?"

*

In the backyard several dogs barked at once. The blind one was teaching them to sing.

The sun had landed. Dark figures stepped out of a door. Shadows were skin. One of them peeled off his face and left it in the grass. The others did the same. It was a garden of expressions.

When I am lost I seek out the most vivid account of the most recent past. In this way, I know I will not over-react.

The figures laughed easily, as if it was over and they were free.

*

The next time in that house, the floorboards creaked. My feet mumbled their misgivings. The boy was a man. He had tattoos, and hair on his chin. In his hands he held a doll. He twisted the doll's neck around and around. Before long he looked up astonished.

He said, "No matter how much I twist, it is not painful."

He went back to his twisting.

The doll had skin. Its eyes bugged.

*

I decided to prove gravity. The flowers had grown since morning. On the roof, I held out my arms. The wind was cool and whisked up my nostrils.

Leaning forward, I mumbled.

The sensation of falling, even from a short distance, parched my bones. Immediately, for the purpose of a bigger high, I considered bridges.

In the grass, I heard bones crack and found faces. I tried one on. My work here was done.

*

Also in the grass, I could feel ants crawling over me. I felt clean. Their tiny feet excited me and my heart soared. A voice in my ear said, "What is a house when it is just a house? What is a house when it is gone? What is the family house when another family lives there now? When what happened inside it is now only inside you?"

Once, a blind dog stepped into my car. She was skinny and pregnant. I cut the cord from around her neck and she licked my face. We talked for hours, and later I would help her with her babies.

I named her something happy. We lived upstairs, near the sun and moon. There was love, in many forms, taped to the walls. People would come in, and immediately give off warmth.

⋆

Fever

Many possible scenarios come together to form a human intellect. Cracks in the windshield spray off in a hundred directions. They said he was never the same.

Memory becomes the smell of scotch in a glass, or is it the smell on a man's breath, which then makes the smell mobile, which then gives the memory feet. For instance, my mood will change if I shave my head.

I will be *different.*

My energy is a function.

My heart beats because it is a machine. For instance, the genitals have more than one use.

Instinct is a word I can wear, a necklace, a string of tin cans over the door. So when an intruder tries to enter, I am warned.

★

A car crashes into a telephone pole. Slick from rain, the highways twist pretty with the color red. In some spots, where the rain gathers heaviest, the red has turned to a pink hue.

It runs like children.

The dampened moonlight gives the picture a frame.

Of reference.

Pulling a body from the wreckage, there is the sensation of cheating death. The sensation sits raw on the nerve endings of my tongue. I wonder if it is my place to interfere.

Minutes later, a woman licks my face. Or is it a dog.

I am no longer in charge of my emotions.

On the drive home, I lost control of my car and crashed into a telephone pole. A woman pulled me from the wreckage. I licked her face.

Later, I informed her I might have rabies.

In a hospital made from straw, a doctor built from bricks breathed into my ear made of wood. I heard three little noises which confused me.

He said the word, "Fever," and put me to bed. At intervals, a nurse came by with needles and cold cloths.

I asked her what day it was. She said, "I am not the angel you asked for."

*

The walls dripped.

I had a visitor, an old man with his hat in his hand. He was accompanied by a woman more than half his age. He was thin, and he trembled.

The woman held his arm.

Stone-faced, he told me, "They said there were no other cars on the road. They said there were no skid marks. You never hit your brakes. They think you were aiming right for it."

I said, "Dad. There is peace now."

*

A dog came to visit. She said on the other side it is confusing. She said she wasn't sure if it was better or worse, but it is different. She told me I shouldn't be so quick to leave. Before sliding out the door, she apologized. "I wish we could have been together longer."

I wanted to see my mother next. But the fever broke.

*

A last nurse came in, trailed by a doctor. She took my blood pressure, while he put his hands on my head. When he wanted to "talk", I knew what kind of doctor he was.

The nurse left.

The door closed behind her.

He smiled and asked me about toasters and extension cords. He wanted to know about pills and "things at home". How is work, he said.

"Stress," he breathed, "is the single biggest killer in America. We do it to ourselves. *Every* death is a suicide."

*

When I was better, I went for a walk one town over. In a little shop I bought magnets for the refrigerator. The magnets had the name *Ocean Grove, NJ* on it. The background depicted various beach scenes.

I needed to remind myself.

I would put little notes on the refrigerator.

Notes like, *I am not hungry.*

Knowledge is dangerous.

My father.

I am sad by nature.

This is real.

At times, my conscience needs a space outside of me.

*

As a woman rang up my purchase, I became curious about her age. Her husband slumped in a chair. Astonished, I said, "He's so much older than you."

She said, "A man in town died."

"What happened?"

She whispered, "Cancer. He was forty-five."

She instructed me to wake up every day hopeful. She informed on her own secrets, revealing the magical aspect of breathing the air, and stretching first-thing.

She said, "In the mornings, I walk outside right away. I like to feel the sunshine on my face. You'll know better when you're my age. We each have only so many days. Tonight, when you go to sleep, there will be one less."

*

I felt the desire to find a reason. That which seemed appropriate behavior yesterday, today felt outdated.

I was getting older by the day.

I have heard this recently, but where?

I have already forgotten. What does this say about my childhood, and how will I ever find my car keys now? Or remember where I left my head, if it wasn't attached to my shoulders?

Which, at times, it isn't.

I feel very simple when I am able to put one foot in front of the other, with no time limit at hand. I need to feel simple.

On the beach, toward dusk, I saw lights. Exploring further, I came to an area where three dogs were lined up. Several adults mulled in the area. They wore nylon coats and thin gloves.

The dogs sat quietly, until a ball was thrown. A man gave a hand signal and the dogs took off running. A woman said, "We are teaching them discipline."

A man said, "We are teaching them speed."

A young child, a girl, said, "The red one is mine."

*

The first dog back dropped the ball at the feet of its owner. He was not rewarded. He was ignored.

The second dog to return was patted on the head.

The third dog returned and was showered with attention.

The dogs were lined up again. The ball was thrown. The process was repeated. The dogs returned in the same order, and received the same acknowledgements.

*

Once more, the dogs were lined up. Once more, the ball was thrown.

This time, the dog who finished last in the previous race now returned first. He dropped the ball, and was ignored. The dog that finished second in the previous race once again finished second, and received his pat on the head.

The dog that had previously finished first dragged in last. He was showered with attention. His ears were rubbed vigorously, and his belly rubbed.

Squirming on his back, all four legs shot into the air.

*

Again, the dogs were lined up. Again, the ball was thrown. The dogs returned in the exact same order, receiving the exact same greetings from the humans.

This was repeated ten more times, until the dogs were breathless. At that point they were given water, and left alone.

A woman said, "We are teaching them to think."

A man said, "We are teaching ourselves. We have learned their personalities. In the beginning, it was a race, and the fastest dog won. But with the reward system now in place, and imbedded in their brains, all that changed. Now it became a matter of personality, and what each individual dog required emotionally in life."

He went on, "After a few races, they found their order. The same dog finished first. We can conclude that he simply likes to 'win', and does not require any other reward than what that already implies. The second dog continued to finish second over and over. In his case, he was happy with a simple brief show of positive reinforcement. Now the third dog, which was earlier established as the fastest, began to come in last each time. This dog basked in the attention he received as a result."

He went on, "This dog understood the rules of the game at first, and chased and retrieved the ball. But when the game changed, he adapted. He began to think it through. They all began to think it through. They balanced out their individual needs, and made *choices*."

Later, this reminded me of when I had lined up people. Instead of a ball, I threw out ideas.

*

A few days later I drove to the crash site. The pole was cracked in half. The town sent me a bill, which I put into a bottle and threw in the sea. The police had questions, which I answered quickly but vaguely.

I said, "I'm not as young as I look. I fall asleep at the wheel."

They drew pictures in a small pad.

I told them, "In my last life I had many diseases which zapped my energy. I am not trying to live forever here. The women I have loved will testify to that."

They showed me the pad. The stick figure was in a "hangman" pose. My next wrong answer would result in the completed picture, and the end of the game. A right answer, though, would keep the game going.

*

A confession
in payments

I let a woman I know, a witch, lay me in my grave. She had lit candles and stripped me naked. It was difficult to move.

I watched her fingers crawl over me. I watched her hand become a tarantula.

I watched myself on television.

*

You could call it a cauldron. You could call them bat wings. You could say she had a way with words when they were grouped together in a certain way. Maybe she chanted. Maybe she spoke in tongues.

Maybe I twitched, there, strapped to a table.

I told her, "I am into pleasure."

She continued to stir me until I boiled, until I smelled good. There were carrots in my ears.

*

By the morning, my wrists burned. The rope was chafing. The wax had dried, and she peeled it much too carefully. On the tip of my penis, first she applied chocolate sauce, and then she applied her tongue, which had been dipped in expensive liqueur.

I could taste neither.

Soon, there was a new ingredient added to the concoction.

*

Later, in chairs, she smoked a cigaret. She said, "I have seen you with your pants down. Where do we go from here?"

She meant, How much more naked can we get?

It was only beginning.

In her mother's house, days later, I sat in a large group of her female family members. My drink was strong and I listened to the conversation. Her mother, a hard woman, stood up. She said, "I am alive in spite of the actions of the men I have tried to love!"

Another woman, an aunt, stood as well. She pulled out a glass phallus, its head enormous. Suddenly it was in her teeth, and then out. When it twinkled in the chandelier light, I winced.

This was noticed.

Soon, I was standing. As one of the few men in the room, I was expected to renounce my kind. Instead, I said, "My cock is a weapon. In the end, you will beg for mercy."

But my tongue was dry, and the words fell like flakes of dead skin.

*

A knife appeared.

I said, "I did not request a vasectomy!"

*

At that, the aunt crushed the head of the phallus in her teeth. In time, it would have melted, as ice will.

She said, "My divorce was a legal action. Governing love has always confused me. My father used to say, Marriage is the reason men die first. My mother used to say, Men don't know what's good for them. I suspect it's somewhere in the middle. But maybe that's too easy."

In the backyard was a fire spit. The tallest among them, her backside a miracle, her front portion a dream, tied me with rope to a cross. In a hood, and trembling, she said, "Christ was a man. This man in front of us must now suffer for his sins."

A torch was lit.

Smack, went the lashes across my back. My erection erupted.

There were dancers, around a maypole.

There were songs, in high-pitched voices.

There were dog-boys and flying monkeys.

There was a fever.

*

The next day, in a ditch, I awoke and staggered to my feet. The dawn never makes accusations – it simply cradles you in its arms. Rubbing my eyes, I attempted to define America. In failure, I approached wisdom, when I said while leaning inside a car window, "I love you."

The car took off, kicking up dust.

What I meant, of course, was, "I am beginning to understand myself."

★

Finally a ride for me – a motorcycle. I held on, well aware I would need to explain myself before it was over. In the diner, the question came.

"How'd you wind up out here, in the middle of nowhere?"

"Women," I said.

"Confuse me," I said.

"At times, when I find myself in their power, the only thing that seems to work as an antidote," I said.

"Is departure," I said.

He chewed his food. His beard had six days on it already.

★

He went into the men's room and never came out. The waitress came by with the check. Her eyes were tired, and drooped down to the floor. She said, "You're not going to stiff me, are you?"

The night before, it was demanded that I confess.

A confession means, Tell the truth.

To the women I had said, "I have never meant any harm. I have always been afraid of you. I see now what that has done to us both."

I hung my head. I said, "I don't have any confidence."

To the waitress, I said, "I don't have any money."

To the cop, from the back of his car, I said, "I don't have a name."

He had wanted identification. But as always I had no proof of who I am.

★

Ambiguous
love child

I felt a strong desire inside me. I wanted to find myself in a stronger position. I decided I needed to act. With my hand firmly around her wrist, I led her into a forest. In a clearing, there was a table set for two.

There was wine in glasses, poured two inches from the bottom.

Music played softly, or the leaves rustled, or it was starting to mist and get dark, or the owls were insistent, or all of this at once. Clouds moved in, dark like small purple hats.

At some point I realized I had it wrong. It was *her* hand around *my* wrist. *She* had taken *me* here. "Tonight," she said. "We finally play house."

*

In her, I saw a kewpie doll with a razor blade smile. I saw a blonde killer with a knife up her sleeve. I saw a killer blonde. I saw a torture chamber in my future.

That torture chamber was called: Permanence.

A life together.

Soon I was in a chair, and there was rope. I tried to move.

Immediately in my mind I tried to forget all the secret information she was about to beat out of me. I did this in a panic. Before I knew it, the questions flew, the bats were loose.

*

"Don't you love me??"

I gulped and spit out the essentials as per the rules of war according to the Geneva Convention. In other words: name, rank, and serial number.

In response, she screamed back nasty remarks about my mother being ashamed. With her eyes clamped tight and squeezing out water, she said, "I already know your name!"

For my rank, I had said, Common laborer for the system.

For my serial number, I said, Four.

I am the fourth child born in my family, in my factory, the fourth model to come along on my particular nuclear-family assembly line.

*

The next question arrived more deviously. "What do you love about me??"

For my initial silence, I paid with a quick snap of knuckles across the bridge of my nose.

"Specifically," she cooed, and then took a long slow pause with knives for eyes. "For your own good, you should think this one over carefully before answering."

Casually, she sharpens the blades. Whistles. Hums. In contrast to my obvious beliefs, I love the dawn and how I am defenseless in its breath.

*

Her third question came at me with blunt force trauma. "Why are you afraid of me??"

I decided I needed to redefine these terms. What is love and death? What is fear and hope? What is truth and beauty? Soon, I realized the entire human language was a farce. I needed to write a new dictionary. I needed to put certain concepts in their place, and put certain others out to seed.

I would need to start with *man* and *woman*.

*

Deeper into the forest, there was another clearing. With my prison shackles on, I hobbled toward it. The pointy stick in my back dissolved any reluctance.

Soon, a picture came into view. Together, we stepped into the frame.

I saw a crib, with a gender-ambiguous mobile sparkling as it orbited. I saw a rocking chair, and lots of powdery wallpaper. In the rocking chair, was a woman. In her arms, was a baby.

I was just getting home from work.

Hoarse, she said, "Don't you have something to say to me?"

I cleared my throat. Ahem. My voice squeaked. "Honey," I said, "… I'm… uh…home."

The hats began to fall and she put one on. Who am I now, she frowned. She said, "You never really want me around. You want me here, but you don't. You make nothing clear. The only thing that *is* clear is you don't know what you want. You're a loner but only on your own terms. That will never be fair to the woman in your life."

I said, "Untie me."

"Untie yourself," she said. "The ropes are in your head."

Later, in a less remarkable setting, we laid together in bed. She smoked a cigaret. "Why don't you want to see me?"

I took the cigaret and dragged it across the room.

Outside, a cat was dying, or car tires were squealing, or the neighbor was playing country music again.

At the window, a drop of rain singed the ash. My arms felt heavy.

I traced my finger along the contour of her body. I used my x-ray vision to see inside to her bones. They were rubbing together, starting fires. I watched her blood pumping. I liked how she was comfortable under my touch. I liked how she cooed with her eyes closed, trusting me.

Stopping at her hip, I let my hand stay on her thigh. I cupped the curve of her body, and rubbed with gentleness.

I felt my hand sink evenly into her flesh until it disappeared completely.

I sunk my penis, and thought I might vanish entirely this way.

Gently, her head rolled off and then back on the pillow. Her eyes retreated even further inside. Her lips pursed tight, locking her smile in, but then her teeth broke free, each one numbered, each one named.

I saw parades.

She hissed, in response to my own method of communication. This consisted of hovering over her, my stupid grin caught between joyous and doubtful as it dangled heavy over her slight jaw-line, all the while my hips thrusting in a continuous precision to her hips circling.

Our eyes were wild. We were sweating.

Finally she said, "You're sending me home again, aren't you?"

The aspirin bottle was on the night-stand. She stretched for it.

I said, "That's not aspirin, is it?"

She popped the lid.

★

Her hair had become straw. Her face had fallen. Her cheeks were only bones now, all flesh was gone. She was a collection of hard angles. For a moment, she was a stranger. She was dangerous.

Her eye-sockets were small dark caves. She swallowed the pills dry, while I listened for the echo.

She said, "I don't like the way you look at me."

There was a cat suddenly, judging us, writing a screenplay.

★

I felt disconnected. I felt like my arms and legs were floating away from my body. I felt like my eyes were seeing things they weren't supposed to see. I felt like a little boy. I didn't have the words to explain what I was feeling. I didn't have the experience.

I said, "I am too young for this."

She stared at me. It was this again. But it wasn't. She said, "I am *not* too old for you. Four and a half years is nothing."

"No," I said. "I mean, we are *both* too young for this. We shouldn't be here yet. It's going too fast."

★

Deciphering my secret code, she re-attached my arms and legs for me. She made my penis work. We were good together like this.

Comfort is a pleasing state of being. It bubbles up quietly from a living surface. The body is a warm twist of muscles. We pull them apart. We stretch each other out, fit ourselves together.

I don't mean aggression, or prowess. I mean being gentle with each other. I mean losing yourself for a while in someone else's perception of you. I mean letting your body talk, letting your movements speak for you. Instinct as a language suddenly familiar.

I mean figuring things out. Letting yourself be figured out. Completely

unraveling. Allowing it to happen.
This is what I mean.

*

Later at the table, she stirred a finger in her coffee. She said, "You know, I'm here a lot. It wouldn't kill you to buy a coffee-maker. You keep the instant around to keep me in my place. You are telling me I am disposable in your life. I'm an instant relationship. Here in an instant, gone in an instant. You keep me in a jar. If you loved me, you would have a coffee-maker."

*

I got up for the window, needing air.
She says, "There you go again. You're always warm. Your blood pressure spikes when you're around me. When are you going to read the writing on the wall. How obvious does it have to be for you."
Her face was lit up, in a playful mode.
I told her she was adorable.
She said, "That would mean so much more to me if you were actually smiling when you said it." But *she* was smiling, and her hand was on my cheek. Her eyes were deep. She was speaking to me from far inside herself, a new place, a hard and real place. She was lost in there, trying to find me.

*

She said, "What if I lived down the road? Or an hour away? Would we see each other more?"
"But you don't."
She said, sighing, "Airplanes are saving us. The Wright Brothers deserve a big fat kiss."
Man and woman. Definitions.
I shook my head. I pulled out the dictionary. I closed my eyes and randomly pointed a finger. You have to start somewhere.

*

Light

Lately I've been slowing down to a stop. Lately I've been living in the rhythm of silence. I can find the cadence, and skip inside it. I can keep up, like a jump-rope. I can concentrate, and be anything. I can keep my feet moving.

I can assume several identities one after the other, all of them anonymous.

I am old now.

But I am new.

*

At a younger age, I had hoped to find someplace loud and raucous. I had wanted to get lost in something I could not control. I was not aware of this at the time. It was instinctual.

So I went to many bars late at night and looked for adventure. I wanted to find the mayhem I needed. I wanted to fight with it in order to fight with myself. I wanted to wake up next to it in order to wake up at all.

I thought having friends would help.

I thought knowing women.

I thought drinking a lot.

I thought if the cops couldn't catch me then no one could.

*

I thought if I didn't stay in one place for very long, then I would never be found. So I traveled. I went across the country. I went to many places in between. I went north and south. I went to other countries.

The most traveling though occurred in my head. Those frequent-flyer miles are still being calculated. It is my belief there is a free trip to the moon in my future.

*

Later on, I thought maybe I needed to slow down, but I didn't know how. So the thought was that I must stop all at once. A runaway train must crash to stop.

This is not good for anyone on the train. This is not good for the train.

*

I wanted to disappear. I wanted to stop talking and stop hearing. I wanted to stop going to my job. I wanted to stop driving a car. I wanted to stop my friends from liking me. I wanted my family to go away. I taught my dog to leave me alone.

I wanted peace.

I wanted nothingness.

I made a decision.

*

At a certain age, you realize nothingness is something too. Also, it is good to be alive.

After ten years, I could find myself in a different place. I could keep myself alive simply by making small minor adjustments as I went along.

This became the key.

Change.

*

I had gathered together the paraphernalia of my emotions. I understood it now. I laid them on a blanket. Earlier, I had run down to the beach before anyone else, and captured the sun.

I kept it now in a mason jar in my apartment.

The glass was warm and bursting with light.

My apartment looked and felt like the surface of the sun. The cats were afraid. I let them outside in order for them to understand their fear. Noting the direction each of them ran, I had some rough ideas about survival.

They didn't run together. One ran this way, one ran that.

The oldest song is, Every man for himself.

*

On the blanket, the assembled equipment had begun to stir. As tiny creatures, they rustled and stretched and crawled. Their eyes weren't open yet. I watched them, kittens, puppies, infants, and when one would crawl too close to the edge I would pick him up and put him back in the middle.

In this way, a living puzzle was being organized. But the pieces were growing, getting bigger. Therefore, the puzzle itself was always changing. This made sense to me on many levels.

She had decided on "love" as her only idea in life. Nothing else mattered to her. Her face was puffy. Her lip was bleeding. On her clothes I could see the harsh element of her journey. In her eyes, I could feel it, like hands around my throat.

Of course I swallowed hard.

She was large eyes sticking out of a head. She was sexy like that. She was drenched to the bone, and her clothes clung to a heaving body. She was sad. "Jane," I said.

I was her last puzzle piece.

But I was growing.

*

We lie in bed, with the covers off, her naked body music next to mine. I was quiet, and listened.

I take my finger and let it hover just above her nipple. If you plucked a hair from my head and tried to slide it between my finger and her nipple, the hair would not fit. I know this to be true.

Yet, I would not touch her.

I would only hover.

She watched me. She tried to figure the equation I was forming in my brain. She knew how my mind worked, and was always ready to believe I was going somewhere with it.

When she breathed, I was on it. On each inhale, I moved my finger just enough to keep the same gravitational pull. On each exhale, I pulled back, again keeping the exact distance. I was locked in.

This went on for hours.

It got dark outside.

*

Finally, she asked.

Pulling back my finger, I was smiling. She said, "What's so funny?"

"I wanted to see how long you would keep it up. I wanted to study your character in a way that would not make you suspicious. Although, your strange look now tells me more about what you think of me than what I think of you."

At this point I shrugged deeply, so deeply that my shoulders touched my ears.

I told her the truth. "I was never cool."

*

Now she took *her* index finger. She traced it around *my* naked body. She said, "Let's draw a circle, and climb inside." She said, "Let's find the silent place we both come from and live there for the rest of our lives."

Later, in the backyard a dog appeared.

"It's the neighbor's," she said. "He likes me."

Dark clouds had moved in, and the wind kicked up. She grabbed my hand, and said, "I have to show you something."

The yard went on for a mile, straight back. We came to a big tree. Apples hung like tiny red-faced men. "It's back here," she said, "where we bury them."

*

I wanted to disappear inside her. I wanted to be romantic about it. Her mouth, first, like a butterfly. Her lips became a consequence.

Sweetness on my tongue.

The meshing of fabric.

Soft skin and hard bone.

The most delicate nerve endings, rubbing together. This is what men and women do when they are alone. Look for themselves in the reactions of each other.

I attempted entrance at several doors. Her eyes locked in on me, while her legs spread, and her aroma welcomed me. What my brain determined in those moments, what my mind forced on my body, is what makes men and women leave childhood so eagerly.

Is what makes puberty the true beginning of human life.

There are no skin frontiers, but the navigational system in our groin is better than a compass. For instance, the sexes are on fire for each other. The heat is a treasure map, and X marks the spot.

I know which way is up.

For instance, nothing matters more to us – in that moment.

But back in our tiny rocket-ship to the stars, back in my apartment the roof was spinning. The sky, she mentioned, can only fall once.

Writhing underneath me, she said, "I have killed my baby before. If you get me pregnant, it will only lead to more of this."

In direct response, I promised her great care and the tidy and safe placement of my ejaculation. I promised myself to remember my heart beating like this.

*

Later, she mentioned how it was strange. She said, "I came here to see you, only to end up in my parents' old backyard. And now here we are back in your apartment. Are we time travelers?"

I told her, "No. We are traveling in the light."

Across the room, she picked up the mason jar, which was dim now. Frowning, she held it out in her hand. The underside of her wrist and forearm made me think of the unattainable, the riddle never solved. "I think it's dead. I think we killed the sun."

Tomorrow, I said. Tomorrow the brown in your eyes will be a road, a dirt road to somewhere just like this. But not like this. Nothing will be dead, but all of it will be dying. And what we say will feel like a hundred years ago.

*

In the morning we took that road to see my friend Dug. There are things you should know before we go any further with this. For instance, I am infatuated by madness. For instance, I pick my friends according to their entertainment value.

Dug proclaimed himself a werewolf and religious wanderer. I had no reason to doubt this, and so was wearing both a cross and my garlic necklace.

Tambourine music made a cobblestone path. I like my feet when they are gregarious. I like myself when I am open to suggestion.

We found him in the yard bent over a water-well. He was pulling on a rope and this action soon brought up a wooden pail. Inside the pail, the water splashed and gurgled. Again, there was music. He put his ear to it, listening to it talk.

It was hot in the sun.

He was slowing down.

He was stopping.

He was listening to himself.

"See," I said to her.

*

In his kitchen, there was a clock that had stopped. It was in pieces on the table. He said, "It would be easy to tell you that I wanted to know how clocks work. The truth is something else though. The truth is I get mad at things that can't get mad back. I consider this a flaw. You can consider it what you want."

He scratched his head.

I scratched mine.

She was wearing shorts and cooking on the stove. Plunge, goes a wooden spoon. And stir, stir. Salt added. Pepper. I liked her like that, different from when she arrived.

I liked me, too.

I stared.

He said, "Now, look. It's not like when I was young. These days you don't have to pick a side. You can switch around a lot. You can change it up."

I said, "It has more to do with our inability to put things into words."

Rubbing his belly, he said, "Forget the words. Turn her over in bed and make her see stars – and make sure you see them, too. Everything else will come from that. But be sweet about it. And if you tell her you love her, you better mean it. That's too hard a place to come back from."

*

About
the author

Joseph Musso Jr. lives in New Jersey,
at a place where the ocean meets the human heart.
<u>I was never COOL</u> is his second book.